I MARRIED A LIZARDMAN

Prime Mating Agency

REGINE ABEL

COVER DESIGN BY
Regine Abel

Copyright © 2021

CONTENTS

I MARRIED A LIZARDMAN

Scaly, grumpy, but oh so cuddly...

As a third daughter on the farming colony of Meterion, Susan's future prospects aren't too promising. A pretty face, top-notch skills, and hard work mean nothing if your dowry doesn't include fertile lands. With her twenty-fifth birthday approaching, and no suitors even remotely sniffing in her general direction, Susan will be forced to leave the family lands to work as an indentured servant in the capital city. Her only way out is to settle for an arranged marriage through the PMA – the Prime Mating Agency. She just never expected to be paired to a grumpy, massive lizardman, and above all not to grow so fond of his scales and quirky ways.

With everything going on, the last thing Olix needs is a mate, especially a squishy, scaleless, off-worlder with strange ways, and an obsession with farming. He is a Hunter, not a dirt digger. The Seer must have been mistaken when she insisted that, for the sake of the people, he take a mate from the stars. How can such a tiny thing be their salvation? And yet, his Susan's softness is disturbingly addictive while hiding a surprising resilience.

With his ancestral lands on the line and the future of the clans threatened, could this wisp of a woman turn their fate around?

DEDICATION

To all those who dare to take chances and aspire to a brighter future. To those who approach challenging situations with an open mind. To those who understand that relationships depend on communication, the ability to listen, the strength to make concessions, and the willingness to try and see things from someone else's point of view.

Whatever our physical differences, the only true barrier that can keep two people apart is the wall we erect in our minds.

CHAPTER 1
SUSAN

I walked fearfully into Kayog Voln's temporary office at the Harvest Fair. Most of the other patrons were indulging in the various treats offered in the many stalls or enjoying the entertainment from live shows and buskers. I was trying to secure my ticket out of the human colony of Meterion. As I had never left my home world, or even traveled to other cities, it frightened me in more ways than one.

However, with my 25th birthday looming dangerously close, I could no longer delay in making a decision. We lived in a matriarchal colony where the first daughter inherited the lands from her mother, and the second daughter served as backup and Superintendent for her elder. It made sense as the second-born had every interest in ensuring the good management of the land that could default to her should anything happen to her older sibling. But a third daughter was merely an extra mouth to feed and too great a risk of more offspring vying for the precious land.

It sucked all the more that, of all my siblings, I was the one truly passionate about farming. They just lucked out in the semen race lottery and were now enjoying a free ride to a life of comfort and security. I didn't hate my siblings, but I might as well have been a stranger to them. In their eyes, I was merely an employee with an expiry date. And that date was coming hard and fast.

I peered around the small kiosk of the mating agency. It looked simple with its white walls, barren but for a giant screen and a small desk with a couple of guest chairs. It had visibly been whipped up quickly and would be taken down just as fast. It didn't try to sell you fantasies or illusions. It was a reality check in a box.

Multiple agencies always attended the fair. The others were fancier, colorful, with the portraits of breathtaking potential part-ners of every species. Over the past four years, their representa-tives had all grown extremely familiar with my face. All of them, but this one, had essentially told me I had more chances of waking up one day with a pair of golden horns and a forked tail, than I had of finding a match. A common farm girl of average beauty, without wealth, minimal education, and not particularly refined or worldly didn't exactly figure at the top of the list of their males looking for a partner.

But this agency ran by the Temern—a bird-like bipedal species with empathic abilities—would not only serve anyone, but always ended up making a match, even with the most unlikely cases. Then again, beggars couldn't be choosers. Most people referred to the PMA—the Prime Mating Agency—as the final stop of the desperate and undesirables. Desperate certainly matched my situation. Undesirables defined the candidates up for grabs. It embarrassed me that I concurred with that definition. I had never considered myself an elitist, but it was true that the species represented by the PMA didn't have people knocking down their doors to be paired with them.

With a name like Prime Mating, you'd think you were getting the best of the best. But in this instance, Prime was refer-ring to the Prime Directive. The agency represented planets still considered primitive but whose population had been exposed to other alien cultures when the Prime Directive had been violated under whatever circumstance. Not only did those species rank low in the technological scale of the galaxy, most of them also didn't quite fall under the stunningly attractive category.

I couldn't wait to see what primitive species, if any, I had been paired with.

Kayog gestured for me to take a seat, the stiffness of his beak-like mouth making his smile fairly discreet. He looked like a bird of paradise with his golden feathers, maroon wings, and a long, fluffy, white tail that reminded me of the train of a wedding gown. His silver eyes observed me with a kindness and wisdom that spoke of his venerable age, despite his youthful appearance.

I settled in front of him and clasped my hands on my lap, feeling both nervous and excited by the news he had for me. When I had received his com requesting for me to drop by, I had known he had something to propose. In my current state of desperation, my answer was already predetermined. The candidate would have to be beyond freaky for me to say no. It certainly helped that, as empathic creatures, the Temern agents personally met each of the candidates to assess their compatibility with the potential partners. I didn't quite know how their psychic power worked, only that whenever they told you someone was a fit, you could be certain that relationship would work out.

"Greetings, Susan," Kayog said with his melodic voice. "It is good to see you so well and under such good tidings."

"*Good* tidings?" I asked with far too much eagerness.

He gave me that stiff smile again which, this time, had taken a sympathetic edge.

"Good indeed," he replied with a sliver of smugness. "I have searched long and hard to find an appropriate match for you. I am happy to report that my search has been successful. He is your perfect partner, although you may not see it at first."

I shifted in my seat, sensing I wasn't going to be too impressed by what would follow.

"The candidate is located on Xecania," Kayog continued. "He is an Andturian Hunter, leader of his clan, and owner of the most fertile lands in the entire solar system."

My eyes widened upon hearing those words, and I perked up, my interest suddenly skyrocketing.

"An Andturian?" I asked.

Kayog smiled again, tilting his head to the side in a fashion reminiscent of the way birds often did when observing something they didn't quite understand.

"He is what you would describe as a lizardman," the Temern agent said, passing his hand over the small holographic display on his desk.

It immediately projected a 3D image of said lizardman. The label had been accurate. Tall, lean but muscular, the Hunter was covered in green and black scales. Although reptilian, his face didn't have the long snout that I expected, but looked rather flat, almost like a human's but without the pointy nose. Two slits served as nostrils. I couldn't quite describe the appendages dangling from his head, almost like scaly dreadlocks instead of hair. Smack in the middle, a frilled membrane started at the back of his head, the length of his nape and down between his shoulder blades. A thick, long lizard tail protruded behind him. Impressive claws tipped the five digits of his hands as well as his webbed toes.

He was naked but for some tribal adornments, a leather harness across his chest, a weapons belt, and a pair of wristbands. Nothing about him screamed wealth or advanced technology.

It is the PMA for a reason.

I swallowed hard while taking in the appearance of the being I would likely be calling husband in the not-too-distant future. Suddenly, all my excitement at discovering a foreign world and about new beginnings filled with hope and possibilities started fading away. Could I truly go through with this? I'd never considered myself a superficial woman, but could I actually mate with a being such as he?

"I can see this was not what you had envisioned," Kayog said in a gentle voice.

My face heated with embarrassment. I didn't mean to appear ungrateful or elitist.

"Do not apologize," he said when I opened my mouth to do exactly that. "He does not correspond to the usual human aesthetic for beauty. Within his people, he is considered a prime specimen. Biologically, both your species are fully compatible. However, his genes are dominant, which mean any offspring you will have will be 100% Andturian in appearance. Although he is a Hunter, the Andturians are a peaceful people. He may not be a fancy match, but he is your perfect match."

"What makes you so sure?" I asked, unable to hide my dubious tone.

"Not only are you the ideal female for him personality-wise, but your background and expertise also make you his people's best hope of survival," Kayog said, his silver eyes suddenly taking on a greater intensity.

My jaw dropped upon hearing this unexpected comment. It also further piqued my curiosity. Finding a mate was my only ticket out of here. But finding a mate to whom I would be valuable could be the recipe for a happy union. Being needed instead of a burden would be such a wonderful change.

"What kind of challenges are they facing?" I asked.

"Financially, the Andturians are poor people," Kayog explained. "The main reason for it is that they don't actually pursue wealth. Over the past couple of decades, an increasing number of foreigners have been settling on Xecania. Its amazing climate, the beauty of its mostly undisturbed landscape, and the breathtaking beaches have made it a very appealing destination for fancy holiday resorts, real estate developers, and venture capitalists."

"And the local population is getting snuffed out?" Although I stated it as a question, it was in fact a bitter statement.

The Temern nodded slowly. "The Andturians are facing an impending famine. In the past two years, they've been having more and more difficulty finding game to hunt when their forests once teemed with life. And the crisis is growing exponentially."

"But I thought you said they had great farmlands?" I argued.

"They do," Kayog said, his eyes gleaming with approval that I'd been paying attention. "One of the greatest appeals of Xecania is its lands. Currently, none of the farmlands are being worked by anyone. And some major corporations are eager to tap into that unexploited wealth. Every report claims that, properly developed, the Xecania food production would by far exceed that of your own homeworld, Meterion. We are talking about billions of credits per year. And it's all going to waste because the Andturians who own those lands are not keen on selling."

"You want me to convince them to sell their lands?" I asked, somewhat confused and slightly outraged.

Kayog chuckled and shook his head. "No, Susan. I want you to convince them to start farming their land and owning this industry on their homeworld. I want you to make Olix and his people wealthier, well-fed, and immune to the bully tactics from the investors and realtors on Xecania. You can turn the tide."

I stared at him for a moment, rendered speechless by this rather tall order. I was a farmer, not a social justice militant. Who was I to try and thwart the plans and schemes of mega organizations? At the same time, we had lived through similar situations on Meterion, with huge corporations trying to acquire our lands. They would have automated the farms with less than ethical methods to increase productivity but in a way that would have not only damaged the land overtime, but also grown products of questionable quality. Being able to help turn the tide would be quite the accomplishment and something to be proud of.

"Why don't they work their lands?" I asked, confused. "It seems like a no brainer to me."

"They're Hunters, not farmers," Kayog said in a strange voice. "For some inexplicable reason, the herds are vanishing. But the Andturians keep trying to track them. Sometimes, people lose their way and need a bit of help finding it again. You can be that guiding light. Don't forget that, as the mate of Olix Nillis, you would own an even greater parcel of land than any of the heiresses here on Meterion, and of far greater quality."

That was a low blow, but an effective one. My whole life, I had dreamt of owning land. This was beyond a dream come true. But at what cost?

"What if I fail?" I asked. "What if they want to keep hunting, and I end up starving right alongside them?"

"As with all the unions arranged by our agency, you have to commit to six months of trying to make it work," the agent explained. "Should the union fail, and you choose to divorce him, we will find you another mate. However, be warned that you will have even less choices than this first time around. As with this union, we will handle all the relocation costs."

Feeling slightly overwhelmed, I ran my fingers through my hair and swallowed hard. This was not what I had hoped for, even though I never really had a clear idea of what I expected. Either way, I would accept. With luck, that decision wouldn't come back to bite me in the ass.

"What's in this for you?" I asked, eyeing him suspiciously.

The Temern smiled. "Our agency works exclusively on behalf of the United Planets Organization. They pay our fees to help grow primitive planets and ensure the locals have a chance at keeping control of their own wealth," Kayog said. "Sending observers and advisors for a few months here and there is usually not very useful. Bringing knowledge and expertise through someone who will become an integral part of their culture bears more fruits in the long term. Your skills can incentivize them to broaden their horizons."

I nodded slowly, understanding the wisdom of his logic. "So, what happens if I agree?"

"Then I will ask you to prepare to leave within 24 hours," Kayog deadpanned.

I gaped at him, suddenly feeling lightheaded. This was moving way too fast. "But... but what of him? Doesn't he have a say in the matter?"

The Temern waved a dismissive hand. "Olix agreed to take whoever would have him. Only your consent is required for this union."

That stung. My already lukewarm enthusiasm plummeted further.

"Wow, is it that bad? I'm not feeling particularly wanted there when my would-be-husband doesn't even care about who he'll be committing to."

Kayog smiled sympathetically in response to my dejected expression. "A Seer told him to marry an off-worlder, and that his mate from the stars would change the fate of their people. He complied."

"If that was supposed to reassure me, it didn't work at all," I grumbled.

The agent burst out laughing. "You know our success rates, Susan. I take great pride in my work and in the happiness of my clients. This may look unappealing to you, and right now you may be feeling rather discouraged, but don't be. Olix is your perfect husband. Trust me, by the time the trial period is over, you will thank me for pairing you with your soulmate."

Despite their undeniable stellar success rates, I had the hardest time believing my fairy tale romance would be with a lizardman.

Nevertheless, I signed.

CHAPTER 2
OLIX

I glared at Molzeg with a disgruntled expression as I prepared to head to the spaceport. The Seer had set me on this crazy path to bond with a foreign mate. I didn't even want a spouse to begin with, not with the countless headaches my people were currently juggling with. But a foreign one?

She looked so strange on the images the agent had sent me. I had seen humans before, but never paid them too much attention. Now, I would be mated to a scaleless female with a skin the color of honey, and head fur the color of turning leaves. How was I even supposed to get aroused by that? Kayog had declared her to be a soft and delicate female but warned me not to be fooled by her weak appearance—she supposedly possessed great internal strength. Time would tell soon enough.

The Seer held my gaze, a mocking smile stretching her scaly lips. According to her, if I supported my human mate, she would drive away the hardships that threatened to destroy our future. Molzeg's foresight was always accurate. Despite the doubts twisting my insides, a part of me rejoiced at this glimmer of hope. And yet, how could a soft human perform such a feat? Did she possess some sort of ritual magic to summon the thinning herds?

Those never-ending questions tormented me during the long ride to the spaceport on the back of my mraka. This place never ceased to overwhelm my senses. Although we used technology in our village, the amount on display here felt excessive. My head spun from all the giant screens with flashy images, various lights each competing for the patrons' attention to draw them towards this shop or this service, not to mention all the voices and music overlapping. Why the off-worlders enjoyed such sensory overload made no sense to me.

Nonetheless, my people were being left behind. We needed to catch up, at least to a certain extent. But we couldn't afford it.

Not unless we sell part of our lands.

I clenched my teeth and silenced the growl that wanted to rise from my throat. The Conglomerate's tactics had grown increasingly aggressive of late. The Natives Council had met a number of times in recent weeks to answer the growing requests for further developments on our homeworld. While we personally would have rejected them all, we couldn't deny the other native species sharing this planet with us the right to explore new opportunities. A part of me wished all those off-worlders had kept flying past our planet. Instead of struggling to maintain our way of life, we would be enjoying the peace our ancestors had fought so hard to reclaim.

As always, the spaceport buzzed with activity, various traders and tourists hurrying past me as they headed towards whatever business was calling to them. The display screen indicated the flight from Meterion had landed more than half an hour ago.

I cussed inwardly.

It arrived early. I hadn't meant for my future mate to stand there idly, feeling abandoned. As I approached the waiting area near the arrivals, my gaze zeroed in on the Temern Agent Kayog and the wisp of a female standing next to him.

I swallowed back the wave of disappointment that washed over me as I seized the opportunity that she hadn't noticed me yet to study her appearance. She was even smaller and more fragile looking than I expected. A twig would likely be sturdier than this female.

Her features did nothing for me. She had tiny brown eyes framing a narrow nose that looked like someone had pinched it then tried to pull it out of her face before giving up. Her lips had an interesting shape and appeared fairly cushiony and plush. Her ears stood out on each side of her face, their round shape giving them an odd appearance while pieces of jewelry dangled from the earlobes. Her head fur shone under the bright lights of the waiting area and cascaded softly down her narrow shoulders.

Although her features looked strange to me, they were symmetrical enough that she probably qualified as attractive for her people. However, her soft outward appearance reminded me of the skin of a plucked bird. How in the world I would lay with this female was beyond me.

But even as these less than charitable thoughts crossed my mind, I realized she would likely be as turned off by my own appearance. If her reaction was anything like mine, despite having seen my image before, I feared reality would hit her hard. Still, she looked demure and poised in her beige outfit consisting of a pair of pants and a long-sleeved shirt. The size of the leather shoes covering her feet only underlined how tiny they were. Swallowing back a sigh, I made my way towards them.

Kayog was the first to notice my presence. Seeing the smile stretching his beak, the female cast a half-startled, half-panicked look in my general direction. Her eyes widened, and she nervously tucked strands of her head fur behind her ear. Just like I had done with her, my future mate observed me from head to toe, doing an honorable job of hiding her emotions. However, the way she swallowed hard led me to believe she felt intimidated by me.

"There you are!" Kayog exclaimed in greeting.

"Apologies," I said in a growly tone, connecting gazes with him for a second before turning back to the female. "Your flight was not scheduled to arrive for another 30 minutes. I had meant to already be here to welcome you upon landing."

"No need to apologize," she said with a surprisingly pleasant voice. "We are early. But I had good company," she added, casting a timid smile at the Temern.

Kayog smiled at the female before proceeding to the introductions. "Susan, this is your mate, Olix Nillis, Clan Leader of the Andturian tribe of the Monkoo Valley. Olix, this is your mate Susan Jennings, third daughter of the Jennings House of the Southern Fields of Meterion."

"It is an honor to meet you, Susan Jennings," I said, pressing my right palm to my chest and slightly bowing my head in greeting.

"The honor is all mine, Olix Nillis," she replied with a slight bow of her head as well, her hands clasped before her.

"Well, now that you've been introduced, we should proceed to the Chapel for the ceremony," Kayog said with an enthusiasm only he seemed to feel. "This early arrival actually plays in our favor in that we can conclude all the proceedings and file your contract with the Registrar before it gets too busy around here."

Feeling awkward, I picked up the small carry-on bag at Susan's feet and followed the Temern. Susan gave me a grateful smile and tagged along, walking on my right. I'd never felt so completely ill at ease with anyone, let alone a female.

It was a short walk to the Registrar's Office. As an increasing number of people had been visiting our planet of late, customs and security had increased to control all the comings and goings. As my future mate, Susan's background check had already been performed by the agency who would also handle all the paperwork. In order for her to move about freely on Xecania, she needed to be made a legal resident. As my wedded wife, she would automatically receive permanent citizenship.

Then again, permanent was relative to the extent that, should she or I decide to put an end to this union within the six-month trial period, her citizenship would be revoked within a week thereafter.

We entered the large room with multiple counters where newcomers had to register and state their business. However, those applicants were still on the secured side of the spaceport with reinforced glass walls dividing the two sections. Thanks to Kayog's presence, Susan had already been allowed through that section but could not exit the spaceport proper without filing her wedding certificate.

We headed to one of the three small rooms at the back. A human magistrate greeted us, standing behind what resembled an altar. A dozen chairs spread over two rows of six, split in the middle to make room for a passage, were the only other pieces of furniture in the room. Apparently, it could be adorned based on the specifications of couples should they so request it. According to Kayog, Susan had been content with the basic setting. I didn't know what had motivated such a choice. A part of me wondered if it was in order to minimize expenses—which shamed me— while another feared it expressed her indifference towards the proceedings—which worried me.

"Susan, Olix, this is Magistrate Elena Mongeau," Kayog said, gesturing at the female behind the altar. "She will officiate your wedding, and I will bear witness. Elena, this is Susan Jennings and Olix Nillis, the betrothed."

We nodded in greeting, and the Magistrate smiled in return. Although she kept a professional expression on her face, I didn't miss the way she subtly eyed me. Curiosity as to what thoughts had crossed her mind clawed at me. Was she wondering why her fellow human would have chosen me?

"Since Olix already informed us that a formal Andturian

wedding will take place in his village once they reach Monkoo, Susan has waived a formal human wedding," Kayog explained. "We will therefore simply do the basic procedures to record a legally binding union as per Galactic Law."

That revelation both took me aback and pleasantly surprised me. Two formal wedding proceedings would have been much in a single day, but I wouldn't have denied her the observance of her cultural rituals. Knowing that Susan had relinquished hers in favor of mine touched me. Maybe there was hope for this couple after all.

"Very well," the Magistrate answered, while taking a holographic card from Kayog.

She inserted it into the slot on the altar before her and rapidly browsed its contents. Visibly satisfied with our respective identifications and wedding contract, she nodded and smiled at us.

"Please stand facing each other in front of the altar," the Magistrate said.

Susan and I complied. My bride swallowed hard again and lifted her head to look at me. Standing face to face only further underlined how small and fragile she looked compared to me. Although she wasn't trembling, Susan's nervousness—or was it fear?—was plain to see.

"We are gathered here to bind this male and female in the legal bond of marriage," the Magistrate said in a solemn voice. "This union is only valid if freely entered into by both partners, not for financial compensation, not through coercion, and not for deceptive purposes. Susan Jennings, are you here of your free will?"

"Yes, I am," Susan replied.

"Do you voluntarily choose Olix Nillis as your lawfully wedded husband, for better or for worse, for richer, for poorer, in sickness and in health, to love and cherish from this day forward until death do you part?"

"I do," Susan said in a surprisingly firm voice.

"Olix Nillis, are you here of your free will?"

"Yes, I am," I replied, my pulse suddenly picking up.

I had never heard the human wedding vows before, but I liked the breadth of commitment they entailed. In many ways, they emulated ours, although we didn't spell them out in so many words.

"Do you voluntarily choose Susan Jennings as your lawfully wedded wife, for better or for worse, for richer, for poorer, in sickness and in health, to love and cherish from this day forward until death do you part?"

"I do," I replied.

"Kayog Voln, Senior Agent of the Temern, do you confirm bearing witness to this female, Susan Jennings, and this male, Olix Nillis, freely exchanging their matrimonial vows?" the Magistrate asked.

"I do," Kayog answered.

"Then, by the powers vested in me by Galactic Law and the United Planets Organization, I declare you, Olix Nillis and Susan Jennings, husband and wife. You may kiss the bride."

My brain froze when Susan suddenly looked embarrassed while staring at me expectantly. The same expression could be seen on the Magistrate and the Temern. Kiss? I wasn't familiar with the term, but it apparently was something I needed to do to conclude this proceeding.

"Hmmm... What is kiss?" I asked, embarrassed by my ignorance.

I almost recoiled in worry when my new mate's skin turned a bright shade of red as she stared at me in disbelief. Why had my ignorance so infuriated her? Was it a sacred part of the human ritual I'd somehow missed in the instructions Kayog had sent?

"Apologies, Susan. I—"

"It's okay," she said, interrupting me, then shrugged while averting her eyes. "It's not important."

I stared at her, feeling at a complete loss. The depth of the red shade of her skin indicated rage in my people, but her voice and body language only expressed embarrassment. Worse still, I couldn't decide whether she was being truthful by saying it wasn't important. Confused, I glanced at Kayog.

"A kiss is a human custom to express affection, among other things," the agent explained. "There are many ways to kiss, depending on if the target is a mate, a relative, or a friend. In this instance, it is tradition for human partners to seal their union by pressing their lips on each other's for a couple of seconds. You only kiss a mate on the lips."

My eyes widened in shock—not to say in horror.

"Why would they do that?" I blurted out, immediately kicking myself for my lack of tact when the redness of Susan's face went up another notch. "Apologies. I am afraid I do not know much about human customs. I promise to do better."

"Like I said, it's okay. Don't worry about it," Susan said, her voice a little more clipped this time.

"I did not mean to anger you," I said, feeling horrible.

"Human's skin turns red for various reasons," Kayog explained in a somewhat amused tone. "Most of the time, it is to express embarrassment or shyness. It is called blushing."

"Oh!" I said, feeling even more stupid for my ignorance. "Our scales darken when we are embarrassed," I said, before snorting while looking down at myself. "As you can see happening right now."

Susan cast a timid look my way, and some of her embarrassment appeared to fade as she took in my darkening scales. The sliver of a smile stretched her lips.

"I will do better to learn of your customs. But for now, if you allow it, I will honor your tradition and kiss the bride," I added.

I wasn't too tempted by that prospect. Why press your mouth onto someone else's? Still, I had just committed to be a good husband to this female for the rest of our lives. Showing some

I MARRIED A LIZARDMAN

respect for her customs was the least I could do, no matter how unappealing it might be.

Now more than ever, I was kicking myself for not reading up on humans. But this whole process had happened too quickly. Only two days ago, Kayog had informed me of a female choosing me, and now she was already here. That had only given me the time to prepare the house for her arrival as well as rush the wedding plans.

Susan hesitated. It bothered me that I couldn't decide if it was because she didn't want me to feel obligated or because she wasn't too keen on kissing me either. I hated feeling so clueless.

"Okay," she said, the redness creeping back around her neck.

She lifted her face towards mine. Bracing, I leaned forward to press my lips against hers. Her pointy nose, oddly pliable instead of hard and unyielding like a fingertip as I'd expected, poked my own. It was an odd feeling, but the softness of her lips against my scaly ones really held all of my attention. It proved to be an unusual but quite agreeable sensation. I lifted my head, startled when the Magistrate and the Temern started clapping their hands. Susan smiled shyly at each of them, but my mind was still stuck on the fact that I wished to kiss her again to better assess that experience.

But that wandering thought was cut short when the Magistrate asked us to sign the wedding contract by pressing our thumbs in the signature box on the interface of the altar. She and Kayog also signed after us in their capacity of witness and officiant.

"Congratulations, Susan and Olix. I wish you a long and happy life together," the Magistrate said.

We both thanked her as she retrieved the holocard from the slot in the altar, which she then handed to Kayog. With a final wave of the hand, she left the room.

"I will go file this with the Registrar," Kayog said. "I'll be back in a moment."

We nodded and watched him walk away. An awkward silence settled between Susan and me. I cast a sideways glance at her only to find her eyeing me. I cleared my throat, thinking how unimpressed my clan would be to see their leader so intimidated by merely conversing with the tiny female he had just married.

"I hope you had a pleasant journey on your way here," I said, failing to come up with a more interesting topic.

"It was very nice," Susan said, looking almost relieved I'd come up with something. "The Agency planned everything perfectly. The accommodations were lovely and so was the staff onboard the vessel."

"I am pleased to hear it," I said with a smile. "You also arrived on a beautiful day on Xecania. It will be perfect for the ceremony in Monkoo."

"I can't wait to see your village and meet your people," she said with a nervous laughter. "I've watched some videos during the trip. Your planet looks beautiful."

"It is your planet and your people now, too," I gently corrected.

"Right," she said, her face heating some more.

It was a fascinating phenomenon. And now, I couldn't help but wonder what other colors humans changed to based on their emotions.

I gestured with my chin at her bag, which I had placed on the floor before the wedding. "Is that all you have brought?"

Susan shook her head. "No, I have many more things," she replied with a sheepish expression that made me wonder at just how much 'many more things' meant. "Kayog says a shuttle will deliver them to the village in 24 to 48 hours. This bag only contains the essentials until then."

"Good. Traveling lighter will allow us to get back to Monkoo faster," I said, relieved.

She slightly recoiled in surprise. "Oh? We're not traveling in a shuttle?"

I shook my head, forcing myself not to show disdain. Granted, shuttles were faster, more comfortable to some—especially elders—and allowed one to carry a lot more at once, but this wasn't the transportation of Hunters, let alone of Andturians.

"We will be riding my mraka back home," I said proudly.

"Is that so?" Kayog said, a slightly concerned look on his face as he returned to us.

"Yes, it's waiting for us outside," I said, disturbed by the Temern's troubled expression.

"I see," he said in a noncommittal tone. He extended a holo-card to each of us. "Here is a copy of your wedding registration and citizenship documents," he added, looking at my mate. "Congratulations to the two of you. I hope we will not meet again, as that will mean a successful union between you. I wish you the very best."

"Thank you for everything, Kayog," Susan said with a grateful expression.

"Indeed," I replied, nodding at the agent.

"Expect your belongings in a day or two, with a little wedding gift from the agency," the Temern added, with a wink for Susan.

"Okay," she replied, her face softening in a way that I found intriguing.

The agent waved goodbye, his wings shifting as he slowly walked away. I turned back to my female, who once more looked uncertain and slightly intimidated. I could understand those feelings. It had to be frightening to uproot oneself and move to a foreign planet to live among strange people of a completely different species.

"Come, my mate. It is time for you to discover your new home," I said, picking up her bag.

She gave me a shaky smile and followed me outside.

CHAPTER 3
SUSAN

As I followed that beast of a male I'd just married, I kept reminding myself that Temerns didn't make mistakes with their matchmaking. I wasn't a social butterfly, but I'd never felt this awkward around a stranger. He knew nothing of humans. Nothing! It struck me once more as pretty reckless on his part to have agreed to marrying a species he was this unfamiliar with. What else was he this frivolous about? On top of that, he didn't seem particularly impressed with me or interested either. Frankly, I rather felt the same about him.

To be fair, I couldn't complain about his appearance. Granted, he didn't exactly fit in my default definition of beauty based on human aesthetic. However, as a lizardman, Olix's features were harmonious. I'd always liked a tall man, and my husband towered over me by a good head and a half. Despite being extremely muscular, he wasn't bulky with excessively bulging muscles as bodybuilders sometimes got. His mostly green scales were quite beautiful, some of them shimmering like emeralds under the sun, while the black scales shone like the finest obsidian. There was something elegant and lethal in the way he walked, silent and fluid like a predator.

During my flight here, I'd read everything I could about the Andturians. Their propensity to walk around naked bothered me to no end. At least, their tails hid their butt cracks and the males had retractable dicks. A good thing, too, considering the decorative loincloth Olix was wearing really didn't hide much. Otherwise, the slightest gust of wind would have exposed the goods. An anatomy essay on the Andturians allowed me to see that the way the scales fell in front of their female's vagina also hid the slit. It wasn't out of modesty but a natural adaptation to prevent unwanted stuff from getting in.

In direct contrast, the farming colony on Meterion was quite prudish. Although it had lost its religious colony status over the centuries, some of the old ways of the Pilgrims had endured. We didn't expose our naked bodies to others, and we didn't sleep around. While purity was no longer a requirement, whether for a male or female, many of us—including yours truly—waited to be married to lie with someone. It was in large part due to the difficulty of accessing contraceptives and the importance of birthright when it came to land inheritance. Impregnating a first or second daughter was a good way for a man to elevate his status and living conditions.

And now, my first time getting laid was going to be with a male who didn't even know what a kiss was. Fan-freaking-tastic…

I wasn't totally clueless. I'd kissed a man or two, given a few hand jobs, although never any blowjobs. But what was my wedding night with Olix going to be like when, by all accounts, his species didn't do foreplay? Their females self-lubricated on demand, and the males usually took their females from behind. They just got straight down to business: wham, bam, thank you Ma'am. I could only hope we'd have some time to discuss the how and why before doing the deed.

Will he even be able to get it up for me, considering how unimpressed he was by my looks?

Being a woman had its advantages. While I prayed he wouldn't split me in half, as long as he was gentle, the burden rested on him. Worst case scenario, I'd just lie on my back, close my eyes, and think happy thoughts while he performed his duty.

However, all such wandering thoughts came to a screeching halt when, only a short walk from the spaceport's main entrance, I spotted a massive beast, looking completely out of place amidst a series of personal shuttles. It looked like the offspring of a razorback mixed with a rhinoceros on steroids. It had the face of a rhino with the two central horns, but the snout of a boar with a pair of extra-long and thick tusks framing its maw. From a distance, its skin resembled the rough one of a rhino, but on closer inspection, it turned out to be thick scales in various shades of light grey to almost black.

The creature's terrifying looks didn't faze me, but the width of its back would have me almost doing the splits. And the pointy ridge of its spine, interspersed with bone spikes—rounded though their tips were—would wreck my hoo-hah and my butt just sitting on it while stationary. I didn't even want to imagine what it would do to my nether region once it started galloping.

I had noticed Kayog's distraught expression when Olix had mentioned we would be riding to his village on a mraka. I had imagined some crazy speeder flying so fast we'd crash into a tree or something. But this?

Olix's proud smile as he came to a stop next to the creature faded the minute he looked at me. I didn't need a mirror to know what horrified expression my face clearly displayed.

"Do not be frightened, Susan," Olix said in a gentle voice laced with worry.

Under different circumstances, I'd be enjoying its deep, grumbling quality, with a slightly sibilant undertone. My husband had a rather sexy accent as he spoke Universal.

"Despite his appearance, Haju is a gentle creature with

people," Olix continued. "He is a well-trained mount and will take us home quickly and safely."

"I... I'm not scared of his appearance," I said carefully. "But I don't see a saddle on his back."

Olix recoiled and gave me an almost offended look. "Only younglings use saddles, and even then, rarely. Do you not trust my ability to remain steady on a mount?"

"Oh, I do not doubt *your* abilities at all," I replied quickly. "But *I* will *never* be *able* to ride that creature as is. He's much too wide for me, and his spine will wreck me down there," I added, my face heating as I gestured in the general area of my nether region.

Olix's lizard eyes widened as he stared at my crotch with dismay.

"Why would it wreck you?" he asked, confused. "Our females ride them all the time without any problem. I will hold you, too."

"Like you, your females have scales down there to protect them from the hard edges and texture of that creature's scales. I'm soft skinned like this everywhere," I argued, pinching the skin of my forearm to show him. "When it starts galloping, it will be like hacking at the meat of prey with a rusty knife, except that meat will be my private parts. It will split me in half, and I will die in horrible pain."

Bewildered, Olix stared in turn at me, my crotch, and the back of the mraka. Disbelief, disappointment, annoyance, and a hefty dose of discouragement fleeted over his reptilian features in quick succession. He emitted a sibilant sound creeped me the fuck out. It reminded me of the hiss of a snake mixed with some sort of a rattling, grumbling sound.

"I'm sorry," I said, feeling horrible as I watched him reflecting on a solution.

He didn't respond, but the look he gave me hurt. And yet, I couldn't blame him for it. I, too, was wondering what the fuck I was doing here. Clearly, I wasn't adapted to this world. Maybe this was happening for a good reason, while we were still at the spaceport. This marriage could be annulled, and I could get my sorry butt back home. I still had a few months before my twenty-fifth birthday.

"Wait here," Olix said in a grumbling tone. "I will find something to make the ride safe for you."

He didn't wait for my response. Turning around, he headed back towards the entrance of the spaceport at a brisk, but stiff pace. I blinked away the prickling in my eyes. I had never felt so useless and inadequate than in this instance. At the same time, I was angry at Olix for not having considered our genetic differences when planning on bringing me home. Granted, he hadn't had much time to look into humans, considering how quickly all of this happened. However, he shouldn't have just settled for whatever species would have accepted him. He should have looked into each compatible one and narrowed the choice down to one he was comfortable with and understood.

And you shouldn't have just accepted him after Kayog had informed you of this.

A wave of distress and sorrow washed over me. I felt increasingly overwhelmed by this whole mess. I hadn't expected a fairy tale, but I had hoped for a smoother start than this—an instant chemistry between us that would have validated the Temern's empathically driven choice of matching us together. But there had been none of this. For him, I was just one big disappointment after another.

Olix never entered the spaceport. Just as he was reaching the doors, Kayog walked back out, carrying something big in his arms. The two males stopped and began to converse. Kayog extended the package to Olix, who took it hesitantly. The conversation between them appeared to intensify, drawing the attention of a few other patrons walking in and out of the spaceport. The Temern gestured with his head for my husband to follow him as they took a few steps to the side, away from prying ears.

My throat tightened. From this distance, I couldn't hear anything they said, but I could see a somewhat concerned expression on the agent's face. Judging by their body language, I suspected Olix was trying to dump me back on Kayog, who was doing his best to convince him to give it a fair try. I felt humiliated and embarrassed. Sure, I might be wrong. Maybe the Temern was only giving him some last-minute advice or insights about dealing with a human mate, but the pessimist side of me expected the worst.

Stupidly, the thought of him wanting to get rid of me suddenly made me want to stay and prove him wrong, prove to him that we could make it, and that I could be the best wife he could have ever hoped for. So much for my own thoughts that this was a mistake.

I wasn't a quitter. His people were going hungry. I could change that. I could be valuable to all of them... if only given a chance.

After a couple more minutes, Olix gave Kayog a sharp nod, and the agent appeared to relax, giving my husband a pleased smile. Olix turned around and started heading back towards me, carrying the package Kayog had given him, while the latter waved goodbye at me. I waved back, tears of relief prickling my eyes.

As Olix closed the distance between us, I recognized the object in his hand as some sort of massive saddle. My heart warmed for the Temern. I cast a glance back at the entrance, but the agent had already left. Of course, he had known it would have been impossible for me to ride the creature and had immediately gone and fetched what I needed. He had made no mystery that he wanted this union to work. But this gesture went beyond the call of duty. I hoped we would make him proud in the end.

"Kayog Voln always thinks of everything," Olix said in a

grumbling tone, showing the saddle in his hands. "This should keep you safe and make the ride enjoyable for you."

"Awesome, thank you!" I said as he began strapping it on the creature.

"Do not thank me, my mate," Olix said, his scales darkening with embarrassment. "It appears that I just keep failing you. I know you are disappointed with how inadequate I am proving to be. But I promise to do better."

My chest constricted hearing the depth of the shame in his voice. This whole time I spent thinking he was judging me and finding me lacking, he'd been beating himself up, thinking I was doing the same to him.

I instinctively placed my hand on his upper arm, giving it a soothing, gentle caress.

"You are not inadequate," I said gently, but firmly. "And you haven't failed me. We are two strangers united by fate, and who have committed to be each other's support and most loyal partner, for better or for worse. You have much to learn about me and humans in general, just like I have much to learn about you and the Andturian people. We can do that together. As long as we communicate and keep an open mind, there's nothing we can't overcome."

His expression softened, and he stared at me in silence, his golden eyes roaming over my face as if he was seeing me for the first time. After a beat, a gentle smile stretched his scaly lips.

"Thank you for your understanding, Susan," Olix said with that adorable accent of his. "I will endeavor to make you proud."

"As will I," I replied with a smile of my own.

My husband made quick work of settling the saddle on the back of the creature. It was quite impressive, with a thick blanket falling to the sides to avoid the scales scraping my legs despite my pants, and an even thicker, cushiony bench that sat on top of the creature's back. It allowed me to sit comfortably with my legs either folded back on each side of the cushion or dangling down. Once he had me settled, Olix hooked my bag to some sort of strap on the front side of the beast. He then hoisted himself behind me, directly onto the unsaddled part of the mraka, and wrapped his arm around my waist. He pulled me backward on the cushion until my back pressed against his muscular chest.

The hard heat of his body around me was surprisingly nice. For some reason, I'd expected his scales to chafe and scrape my skin, but they felt oddly supple against me. Despite the elevation provided by the saddle, Olix still sat almost a head higher than me. His pleasant earthy, woodsy scent titillated my nostrils. Cocooned and sheltered by his body, I relaxed against him.

"Is this comfortable for you?" he asked, his deep voice giving me goosebumps.

"Yes, this is perfect. Thank you," I replied.

"Good. I will go slowly at first. If you start feeling pain or discomfort at any time, please let me know immediately," he said.

"Okay," I answered, feeling touched by his solicitude.

We began to ride mostly in silence, the mraka gradually picking up the pace. Within ten minutes, the beast was galloping at dizzying speed. At first, my stomach roiled a little, and my teeth chattered, but I eventually adapted to the motion, flowing with the creature's movements, as well as Olix's behind me. I would still be sore as all hell in the morning, but in time, I didn't doubt for a minute that this method of transportation would grow on me.

Although Olix pointed out some landmarks along the way, he mostly remained quiet. I didn't mind. Between enjoying the stunning view of the mostly untouched, savage land, I welcomed this opportunity to gather my thoughts and mentally prepare for meeting his people... *my* new people.

After an hour's ride, I almost asked for a break as I was beginning to feel cramped, tired, and thirsty. However, as if he'd guessed my growing discomfort, Olix announced we were less than ten minutes away. I decided to keep quiet and suck it up.

To my delight, the silhouette of the village finally appeared on the horizon. I'm not sure what I had expected, but not the elegant structures of stone, wood and glass that greeted me. The dark browns and light beige gave it a warm and peaceful aura. The harmonious layout of the village spoke of well thought out urban planning and ingenious design that married the modern elements of the constructions to the natural environmental setting.

The one-story dwellings surrounded a large stone plaza at the end of which a massive building sat. It had to be their gathering hall or serve in some sort of official settings. While most of the village appeared to be covered in packed dirt, some cobblestone paths indicated the main 'roads' if that term applied. At a glance, I estimated the village contained a couple of hundred houses surrounded by vast plains on each side, a dense forest in the short distance, and a wide river at the back.

The absence of fortifications or defensive walls around the village spoke volumes about the peaceful nature of the inhabitants of both this area and of the planet as a whole. While the Andturians relied heavily on hunting and—to a lesser extent—fishing, no dangerous predators roamed nearby.

But as we closed the distance with my new home, my innards twisted in a knot at the sight of dozens—if not hundreds—of Andturians of all ages gathering on the plaza to witness our arrival.

"Calm, Susan," Olix suddenly said next to my ear as he began slowing down the speed at which the mraka galloped. "These are your new people now. No one will harm you. You are among family and friends. They look forward to meeting you."

I couldn't tell what gave away my nervousness, or if he was just anticipating what emotions might course through me at this time, but his words helped alleviate part of my stress. I would likely remain a complete mess for the next few days, but every bit of support was welcomed.

"I hope they won't be too disappointed," I mumbled, immediately kicking myself for it.

But his answer took me aback.

"No, my Susan," Olix replied in a strangely serious voice. "It is *we* who hope *you* will not be too disappointed with your new home and people."

For the first time, I wondered how they might all be feeling at the thought that I would be judging them as they would be judging me. Did my opinion really matter to them?

Olix is their ruler… or rather Clan Leader.

Yes, I could see how they might want to meet the approval of their leader's wife. But it also struck me that, as such, I would fall under even greater scrutiny. How humiliating it would be for him if his 'subjects' found his 'queen' pathetic? I didn't want to embarrass him or cause his authority to be undermined.

That thought gave my already knotted stomach another nasty little twist.

But all meanderings fled my mind as our mount came to a stop under the cheers and the greetings of the clan. I didn't know where to look with so many lizard faces surrounding me. To my shame, if not for the different colors and patterns on their scales, I would have been hard pressed differentiating them. They all looked the same to me, except for the noticeable size and shape differences that separated the two genders. Although my brain recognized variety in their features that made each face unique, it would take it a while to process this information overload.

Olix deftly jumped off the mraka then lifted me from the saddle as if I weighed nothing before setting me on my feet in front of him.

"Susan, this is the Monkoo village, your new home. And this is my clan, your new family," he said, gesturing at the people and the village in general with a wave of his hand. "People of

Monkoo, I present to you my human mate, Susan Jennings from the Southern Fields of Meterion."

They all slapped their tails on the ground twice while pressing their right hand to their chests in a welcoming gesture. Feeling super awkward, I responded with a stiff smile and an even stiffer nod of the head. Although none of them displayed open hostility, by the way they subtly assessed me, none of them seemed particularly impressed. I had my work cut out for me to prove my worth.

Two females approached us, one clearly older, judging by the thickness of her scales, almost the same hue as Olix's, the darker color of the strange strands that made me think of braids on their heads, and the number of beads and knots in the tribal jewelry she wore. The other female, visibly younger, but still of adult age, had stunning, blue scales that shimmered like gems under the sun.

"Susan, this is my mother Yamir and my younger sister Luped," Olix said.

"Welcome, Daughter," Yamir said in a surprisingly welcoming voice.

"Welcome, Sister," Luped replied with excitement that made me instantly like her.

I mumbled back a greeting. I didn't know how sincere their welcome was, or how they felt about me as a wife to Olix, but this initial greeting made me feel much better... less alone among strangers.

CHAPTER 4
SUSAN

I nearly panicked when both females each grabbed onto one of my upper arms and started luring me away.

"We have to prepare you for your mating ceremony," Yamir said while pulling me after her.

I cast a worried look over my shoulder toward Olix who smiled encouragingly while getting himself dragged away by a couple of males.

"Do not worry," Luped said as I followed them, trying not to freak out. "We are just going to adorn you in the traditional colors, then we will bring you back to the square... hmmm... plaza I think you call it. There, our Seer, Molzeg, will bless your union. And then, we will feast and dance!"

I knew a second wedding ceremony awaited me upon my arrival, but I thought they'd grant me an hour or so to relax, stretch my legs, guzzle down a drink, unpack my stuff, and get my bearings. I didn't even get a chance to take my bag from the mraka.

"I do not mean to be rude," I said as the two females ushered me inside a beautiful dwelling right next to the plaza and which seemed a bit more imposing than the others, "but, may I ask what's the rush? I've only just arrived."

Thankfully, neither female appeared offended by my words, an air of sympathy settling on their alien features.

"I am sorry you feel this is rushed," Luped said. "It must be overwhelming for you. However, many of the guests come from neighboring clans. They have made a long journey here to pay their respects and honor your union. They must return to their respective villages after the celebrations. As we travel in the traditional fashion, it would be more challenging for their young to travel after nightfall."

"I see," I replied, both flattered and mollified by her answer. "I had not realized neighboring villages would go through such trouble for my wedding."

"Of course, they would," Yamir said with a slight frown. "You are marrying the great Hunter Olix Nillis, Leader of Clan Monkoo. He is the Spear of the Andturian clans of Xecania. He unites us all. Any less would have been an offense to him, but especially to you."

These words felt like a warning but also like a major burden had suddenly been rested on my shoulders. The way she looked at me as she spoke them clearly meant to convey the fact that I now had a duty that would impact her son's standing among his people, both here in our village and amidst the other clans. I had not bargained for that.

"I am honored," I replied in a small voice.

That answer seemed to please her. Smiling, she lured me closer to the large table that occupied one half of the vast room that seemed to serve as an open plan dining and living area. There was no kitchen per se, only what could amount to a kitchenette at best. Andturians were a community-focused species and didn't cook individually, but for the clan as a whole. At the back, a series of doors led to what I assumed to be bedrooms and storage space.

Massive windows ate up most of the walls of the main area. While they gave us a clear view of what was happening outside, they didn't allow people outside the house from seeing within. And it was a damn good thing, too, considering my mother-in-law immediately began trying to rid me of my clothes.

It was highly uncomfortable, although not unexpected. As Kayog had warned me of my Andturian wedding, I had read up on it on my way here. As with everything else, their people didn't wear clothes. In the meantime, Luped was mixing some sort of tribal paints that they would apply on me.

"So… regarding the wedding attire," I said tentatively, while allowing Yamir to help me out of my shirt and pants, "my people are not comfortable with full nakedness like yours."

Yamir stiffened and stared at me, my pants clutched in her hand. I licked my lips nervously, cast a sideways glance at her daughter, who was also looking at me, before pursuing my thought.

"I don't need to tell you that, unlike Andturians, humans do not have scales," I added with a nervous laughter. "Our clothes do not only shelter us from the cold and from getting hurt by things we might come into contact with, but they also helped preserve our modesty."

"Modesty?" Yamir asked, tilting her head to the side.

"Our anatomy is different," I said, choosing my words carefully.

I didn't know how much they knew about humans. I always felt it was better to err on the side of caution but also didn't want to offend them by stating the obvious or implying that I questioned their intelligence.

"You do not have prominent breasts like human females do," I said, gesturing at my rather generous boobs. "Although our lower region is generally similar," I added waving at my crotch, "yours is naturally covered and protected by scales. Mine is completely exposed, as is my behind."

My cheeks felt on the verge of bursting into flames from embarrassment. I couldn't believe this was the first conversation I was having with my in-laws. What the heck had I gotten myself into? And yet, I forced myself to plow through.

"My people were originally a religious colony. It was considered a crime to expose our nudity to any male other than our husband, or a medical professional for the purpose of treatment. While it is no longer a crime, we still consider it inappropriate to expose ourselves in public, especially to people of a different gender. My husband is the only man that should see me naked."

To my surprise, the two females had taken on a wary expression, Yamir in particular, taking a few steps back as if she was becoming afraid of me. It wasn't fear but concern of what I might do. My brain froze for a second, and then it hit me.

"Is my face red?" I asked, touching my cheeks, the heat confirming I was probably beet red.

"Yes," Yamir answered carefully.

"I'm not furious," I said with a nervous chuckle. "Olix thought the same earlier. Humans take on various shades of pink and red, around our faces and necks, when we are very shy or embarrassed. We can turn red when we're angry, too, but then it is very obvious that we are furious. We're usually shouting and grimacing when that happens."

Yamir's and Luped's shoulders relaxed, a relieved expression settling on their faces.

"Thank you for this explanation, on both your people's culture and your anatomical responses," the older female said. "We were getting afraid we had somehow provoked your ire. When our people's scales turn this shade of red, a bloody battle usually ensues. I would have hated to have to explain to my son why we were facing off in a duel with his new mate."

This time, I couldn't help but chuckle at the visual. Then again, it would not have been amusing for me as the females were clearly quite strong—almost at par with their males according to what I had read—and would have made mincemeat out of me.

"It would have indeed been quite awkward," I concurred. "However, I understand that you are now my new people, and I want to at least meet you halfway when I cannot fully embrace some of your ways. I cannot show my private parts in public, as we call them, but I can wear certain underwear that will at least give the illusion that I am. But for that, I would need my bag that was left on the mraka."

"I will go get it," Luped offered with an enthusiastic smile.

Without waiting for my response, she headed straight for the door. I barely had time to thank her before the door was already closing behind her. I turned back to my mother-in-law to find her smiling oddly at me.

"I did not know what to think when Molzeg insisted that my son, our leader, should take an off-worlder as his mate," Yamir said as if musing out loud. "I feared you would trample every single one of our ways and entrench yourself in your own, which would inevitably undermine my son's position, especially considering these trying times. This consideration you are showing to our culture, while remaining true to yours, honors both our peoples and gives me hope for the future. A clan leader's mate naturally has greater responsibilities. As a foreigner, you will sustain even greater scrutiny. As long as you maintain this open-mindedness and willingness to uphold our values to the extent of your capacity, you will find me a loyal ally."

Those words moved me more than I could express. However, I didn't get a chance to respond as Luped stormed back in, showing me my bag with a triumphant grin. I smiled at her mother and nodded to express my gratitude at her words before thanking Luped.

I fished out my nude underwear from the bag, the finest lingerie I possessed, aside from the black lace set I had also acquired for my wedding night. I had bought both before my departure, which had earned me some pointed looks from the clerk on Meterion.

As I held the lingerie in my hands, I looked in turn at the two females who were staring at me expectantly. Heat creeped back onto my cheeks when I realized they were waiting for me to strip in front of them. It was odd that I should feel so self-conscious when I had undressed countless times in front of other women without a blink. But them being alien made things completely different.

A part of me wanted to sneak into one of the bedrooms to change. After all, I had just given them the whole speech about us not stripping in front of strangers. But I had specified that it mainly applied to not showing ourselves to other males. Swallowing back a sigh, I decided to suck it up and just finish stripping, more grateful than ever that I had smoothly shaved all the bits that needed to be.

While my breasts certainly piqued their interest, my hoo-ha acted like the world's biggest magnet. The way their lizard eyes zeroed in on it, you think some sort of neon sign pointing at it was blinking frantically, commanding their attention. I'd never felt so embarrassed in my life. You'd think I was some sort of insect being studied under a microscope. I didn't doubt for a minute that the females meant no disrespect. In their stead, I would have been fighting like hell not to stare, but my eyes would be fighting me tooth and nail to keep peeking.

Judging by their oddly expressive faces—which I had expected to be stiff with all those scales—they were quite taken aback by its appearance. Needless to say, I worried about my husband's reaction when the time would come. Either way, I quickly slipped into my undies to put an end to that scrutiny. And yet, even after I had put my panties on, the females continued staring at my crotch for a short while longer, as if they could see through the fabric, while I donned my bra. I still felt far too naked and exposed, but I consoled myself by trying to imagine this was a bikini and not underwear.

Nevertheless, the color did blend well with my skin tone, and both my in-laws appeared to approve of the final result. They immediately proceeded to draw swirly tribal patterns on my arms and neck with the paint Luped had mixed. They worked with a swiftness and an exquisite dexterity that left me breathless, especially Yamir. To my pleasant surprise, the paint didn't have a chemical scent, but a lovely spicy-sweet aroma that reminded me of mulled wine.

Once that task was completed, they adorned me with bracelets and necklaces of incredible craftsmanship, but then appeared completely baffled when it came to what to do with my hair. The thick but supple strands, covered in some kind of thin scales, that dangled at the back of their heads reminded me of strange dreadlocks. It would take far too long for me to braid my hair in a way that even remotely resembled that, but I had smart rings that would automatically spiral around the length of however thick the section of hair I clipped it around. The coppery wire looked beautiful against my hair; their color almost similar.

Yamir's eyes widened with surprise and then pleasure when I did the first one. Luped made a weird hooting-hissing sound of approval as I moved on to the second. Within minutes, I'd done my whole head with two dozen faux dreadlocks. Normally, I only did one on each side of my face, like the Vikings of old would have a pair of braids framing their faces. Luped and Yamir tied a few leather strings to my locks, from which dangled various small, colorful, polished stones.

By the time they were done, my head felt a little heavy, but not painfully so. Ready at last, the females gestured for us to go. To their dismay, I retrieved a pair of simple pair of slide sandals and shoved my feet in them.

"My soles aren't protected like yours," I explained. "I would hurt my feet and likely cut myself on the small rocks on the ground."

The females both looked at my feet, once more unimpressed by how squishy I was turning out to be. Their scaly lips quivered in what I assumed to be the equivalent of a human pinching her lips reprovingly. Thankfully, they did not give me a hard time about it.

Yamir gestured for me to head towards the door. Granted, a good half hour had already gone by since we'd entered the house, probably even more. However, as the Plaza had been mostly barren upon our arrival, I expected the people would want a bit more time to finish setting things up, whatever they would be. To my shock, as soon as Luped opened the door, I was greeted with a mesmerizing view of my wedding altar.

Instead of the traditional chairs and benches, and excess of flowers and ribbons common to human weddings, the Andturians had laid out rows upon rows of low, cushioned benches, in a circular radius on the plaza. Right outside the last row, evenly spaced tiki-looking torches surrounded the area. Floating lanterns created almost a starry dome overhead. Clearly, no technological device operated them. It took me a moment to notice the barely visible network of thread that connected them, keeping them from flying away.

In the center, the elder female named Molzeg awaited us. A small, cylindrical altar made of some sort of lightwood, carved with the most beautiful and intricate design, sat in front of her. Behind her, two impressive males held what I could only presume to be ceremonial objects.

Mesmerized, I advanced almost in a daze while the people began chanting and making rhythmic sounds with both their hands and their tails. It took me a moment to realize that Olix was on the other side of the plaza, straight in front of me, also being escorted to the altar, but by two males instead.

I didn't know him, and I certainly wasn't in love with him,

but the hypnotic sound of the percussion instruments, of the alien voices chanting, of their rhythmic clapping, and the beauty of these simple decorations put me into a magical trance that I only expected to experience in a marriage of love. My heart fluttered, and my head spun as I put one foot in front of the other.

We stopped in front of each other, eyes locked. Something strange passed between us. I was so lost in the moment that I didn't even notice the chanting stopping and the Elder Seer beginning to speak. The sight of a light smoke floating between us with a scent of herbal incense snapped me out of my daze. I then glanced at the altar where some herbs were burning while Molzeg recited the traditional speech of the Andturian weddings in their native language.

I did not have the translation module for it. It was never built due to the lack of demand. Andturians were still considered a primitive species and had a fairly small population that mostly kept to itself. As they spoke Universal pretty well, it was never deemed necessary. At least, my translator would eventually learn their language.

Despite my lack of understanding of the words themselves, I basically imitated whatever Olix did. When Molzeg presented him with a plate containing a dried fruit that reminded me of a prune, he picked it up and brought it to my lips. I accepted the surprisingly tasty morsel and ate it. Then I reciprocated by feeding him a similar thing. When he extended his hands towards me, palms facing up, I placed mine in his. Molzeg then took a bowl from one of the two males behind her then began circling around us, dipping her fingers inside it, then splashing us with some droplets. The whole time she chanted something to which the assembly responded a single word with religious fervor.

I had no clue what that liquid was, but it looked clear like water and had no particular scent. Then again, with the herbal incense still burning, it would be hard for my poor human nose to detect anything else, unless it was very pungent. The Seer completed three such rotations around us before remitting the bowl to one of the males. She then turned to the second male and took from him long leafy branches.

Once more, Molzeg circled around us, brushing the leaves over Olix's back down to his thighs, then back up his sides to his shoulders, before following the length of his arms. Pursuing this path, the branches caressed my hand, still held in his, and repeated the pattern in reverse, up my arm, down my side, over my back and then along my other arm until it reconnected to Olix over our other hands.

Although I couldn't be certain, I believed this was a ritual of binding. It was rather pleasant and beautiful, bringing a smile to my face. Then Molzeg stood next to us. She placed the leafy part of the branch over our joined hands and said something else at the end of which Olix responded with a single word. Panic immediately set in as I hadn't understood the word and would never be able to repeat it. My breath hitched when Molzeg turned to me.

"Are you freely taking this Hunter to be your life partner, the sire of your offspring, the pillar upon who you rely in your moments of weakness, and do you promise to be his safe haven at all times and the rock that will help him stand tall when his own strength wavers?" the Seer asked in Universal.

"Yes, I do," I replied, relief flooding through me.

In response, Molzeg slapped the leaves over our hands. As mine were on top, it stung quite a bit. Not enough to hurt, but enough for me to notice. She recited a few more words then flicked the branches again in quick succession over Olix's fore-arms and then over mine. This time, I flinched and clenched my teeth. That one hurt. Olix noticed my change in demeanor and slightly frowned, a questioning look in his eyes. But I never got a chance to even try to express the source of my discomfort.

I heard the whistling sound before the branch connected with

Olix's side. He didn't flinch or even seem to feel it. My stomach dropped, and my blood turned to ice as the whistling sound—frighteningly reminiscent of that of a whip—resonated again seconds before the branch connected with my bare waist.

Searing pain exploded in my side, and I cried out. Yanking my left hand out of Olix's, I covered the wounded area while casting an outraged and disbelieving look at the Elder Seer.

"What the fuck? Ow! Be care—"

"NO!" Olix shouted, interrupting me. The look of shock and horror on his face instantly numbed the throbbing in my sides. "What have you done?!"

An ominous silence had settled over the gathering, the same horrified or crestfallen expressions reflected on every face. The way they looked at Olix's empty hand as one would the boogeyman, I realized I'd royally fucked up.

CHAPTER 5
OLIX

I couldn't breathe, I couldn't think. A single thought kept replaying in my head: she had broken the circle. And yet, underneath it, fighting for dominance, lurked another thought: my mate had been hurt. The cool breeze on my empty hand felt instead like the scorching heat of a thousand fires. With that gesture, in that split second, Susan had cursed us to a broken and miserable union. Her being a stranger had already been a challenge that the people had accepted with a bit of reluctance. But now, they would never acknowledge the authority or legitimacy of a Clan Mistress anointed through a doomed union.

It was all the more heartbreaking that, judging by her expression, she had not known.

"All is well, Olix Nillis," Molzeg said in Universal, in a calm but loud voice so that all would hear. "Take back the hand of your mate and reform the circle. She did not deliberately sever it. My clumsiness caused it."

Maybe so, but the circle had still been broken. It had to be a sign from the Spirits.

"The circle was broken," Zoltar argued from his seat, a couple of meters from us.

A few others in the gathering nodded their heads with a troubled expression on their faces.

"The circle was *not* broken," Molzeg said in a stern voice, glaring at him. "It was breached, yes, but never broken. Her right hand, the one that holds the foundation of their union, never parted from him. This means they will face difficult times—as is to be expected when mating with an off-worlder—but their roots are strong enough to withstand and vanquish the storm."

My lips parted as I gazed at her right hand that had indeed remained tightly bound in my left. In fact, when Susan had felt pain, the grip of her right hand had tightened, as if seeking strength and comfort from me. Relief flooded through me. Although I couldn't yet see it, and new though it was, this was proof that we indeed had a strong foundation. Difficult times, I could weather.

Zoltar harrumphed his doubt, but the Elder Seer's words appeared to mollify the others. Susan was looking at me like prey cornered by a predator. Guilt and fear shone bright in her brown eyes. I extended my right hand again to Susan. The eagerness with which she grabbed it, and the relief on her face almost made me smile.

Yes, we were strangers, and both had doubts about the other but, like me, Susan truly seemed to want this to work. We would find a way.

Molzeg resumed the ceremony, expediting the rest of the process. This time, she barely brushed the somitan branch over my mate. That idiot Zoltar would never let me hear the end of what a weakling my female was. The swipe that had made Susan cry out would have barely tickled a youngling. And yet, I could see the angry welts already rising on her skin where Molzeg had struck.

How could such a fragile species have survived this long and even grown to be far more advanced than ours?

Still, our union ritual shouldn't have caused her pain. My

protective instincts wanted to take her to our dwelling and apply soothing ointment on it. Thankfully, this was coming to an end, but I expected Susan would balk some more about the next step.

Molzeg separated our hands before handing a dagger to my female. Susan eyed it with complete confusion.

"Andturians bite each other to seal their union," the Seer explained. "The mating bite is not only a visible symbol to all that the person is bound, but our saliva also contains healing agents. The exchange reinforces each partner's immune system. Your teeth are too blunt to pierce your mate's scales, since they are the thickest around our necks. You may therefore use this dagger."

The horrified look on Susan's face both embarrassed and irritated me. Was everything really this overwhelming to her? I wanted this union to work, but it seemed like every other moment pointed out another reason it couldn't. I was beyond ready for this ceremony to be over.

"You want me to stab him in the neck?" she asked, disbelieving.

"Yes," I replied in a slightly clipped tone.

"But… but I could seriously harm you," she stuttered.

"No, you won't. Go ahead," I said, trying to speak patiently.

Susan tentatively raised the dagger, her hand shaking. When she hesitated a moment too long, I gave in to my annoyance, closed my hand over hers, and stabbed at the fleshy part of my shoulder. She gasped in fright when the tip sank in. I yanked it back out, barely bothered by the sting.

"See? It wasn't that hard. Now, you must lick a drop of my blood off the blade," I said, praying that she wouldn't make another fuss.

This was becoming beyond humiliating in front of all the clans. To my relief, she complied. However, guilt quickly replaced it. Susan was visibly shaken. I didn't think she had licked the blood willingly, but more in an automatic fashion, shock making her simply go through the motion. I was making a complete disaster of things. I should have had my mother prepare her better for this.

"I will now bite you," I said, my voice coming out a bit rough due to guilt. "It will not harm you. There will only be a little sting."

She nodded, her eyes wide as saucers. I placed my hand on the left side of her neck before leaning in to bite the right side. My innards twisted when I felt her trembling beneath my touch. The slightly acrid scent rising from her skin confirmed she was indeed either frightened or traumatized. I was a failure as a mate. She had looked so mesmerized and enchanted when the ceremony had begun. And yet, I had managed to ruin both her human and Andturian weddings.

Swallowing down the bile of shame rising in my throat, I gently caressed the side of her neck with my thumb in what I hoped to be an appeasing gesture. Not wanting to prolong her discomfort, I summoned the healing fluids in the sac at the back of my throat then quickly bit her, making sure not to sink my teeth in too deep in light of how fragile her skin was. She stiffened at the sting but didn't otherwise react.

I licked the wound, the iron taste of her blood lingering on my tongue. Within seconds, her eyes widened, but this time with awe as the healing fluids in my saliva sealed the wound, keeping it from bleeding further and numbing the area.

"You are officially mated before the Spirits and the Andturian people," Molzeg declared. "Welcome to our family, Clan Mistress Susan."

The people tapped their tails and whistled their welcoming chant. This was finally over. I turned to the people and tapped my tail twice on the ground while pressing my right palm over my heart. Susan eyed me before repeating the gesture, tapping the ground twice with her right foot instead.

It was beyond adorable.

Everyone started laughing, but not in a mocking way. Despite the earlier incident, approval shone on their faces at her attempt to adapt to our customs and working around her limitations. That instantly lightened the general mood, and she gave the audience a timid smile, a pale redness creeping back on her cheeks.

Thankfully, while she'd come fetch Susan's bag, my sister had the foresight of warning my people of the meaning of a human's reddening skin. Therefore, no one panicked and instead observed the phenomenon with undisguised curiosity.

"Come, my mate," I said in a gentle voice, placing my hand on her back to nudge her forward. "We will go to the Great Hall for the feast."

She hesitated and gave me an uncertain look. "Would it be okay for me to put some clothes on, now? It's a little chilly, and I'm getting cold."

Her redness increased again. And then she shivered, and a swarm of bumps erupted all over her skin.

"Are you unwell?" I asked, instantly worried.

"No, no! It's just goosebumps. That happens when humans get cold or when we feel certain types of emotions," she explained sheepishly. "It will fade away in a few seconds."

My mother coming to stand next to us with an inquisitive look on her face put an end to that topic.

"Susan is cold," I explained to my mother. "Her skin requires clothes to maintain a healthy body temperature."

My mother's eyes widened in understanding. "I will take her to your dwelling so that she can dress. You attend to your guests," she replied.

"Thank you, Mother," I said, affectionately.

Susan's relieved and grateful smile made my chest tighten again. She was making many sacrifices for me, and I wasn't taking good enough care of her. Once this evening had concluded, and our guests had departed, I would start doing better by her.

"Please tend to the welts on her sides while at it," I added in Andturian.

"Of course," my mother replied before ushering Susan home.

I watched them walk away until they entered my dwelling. Luped's hand on my shoulder brought my attention back to my immediate surroundings. Smiling, she gestured with her head at the Great Hall. I smiled back and walked alongside her, accompanied by the other guests. As soon as I entered the building, my heart filled with gratitude for my people. Despite the scarcity of food, all the clans had contributed to give us an impressive feast.

I did a quick round of the many tables surrounded by circular benches where the clans had taken their places. In the center of the room, a large warbull had been roasting on a spit alongside a couple of boars, and smaller game meats. Various roots and vegetables wrapped in giant leaves were cooking near the coals. Gatherers from all clans were beginning to carve the meat so they would be ready to serve the meal once my mate had returned.

After expressing my thanks and paying my respects to the other clans, I made my way to the main table at the back of the room. Unlike the others that were circular, this one was long, narrow, and rectangular. It had benches only on the far side so that the people sitting there could face the other guests in the room. While my council usually shared that table with me, today, only my female and close blood relatives would.

Naturally, I didn't make it there without getting intercepted by Zoltar. The male was becoming a thorn in my side. There had always been a healthy competition between us, ever since our childhood. He had wanted to be clan leader in my stead—and still did—but acknowledged that I was the better Hunter. However, since the game had increasingly been deserting our hunting grounds, Zoltar had begun challenging me more often and more vocally. He believed his ideas on turning the situation around would work better than mine. Molzeg's insistence that I mate with an off-worlder to help save our people had only rein-forced his belief that I was no longer suited for the role.

In his stead, I would probably feel the same.

Zoltar wasn't a bad male, just too impulsive and headstrong. He was a great Hunter but would make a terrible clan leader.

"Well, that was an interesting spectacle," Zoltar said in a taunting voice. "You mated a plucked bird more brittle than a twig."

"Watch it, Zoltar," I snarled, taking a menacing step towards him. "It is my female you are speaking of and your Clan Mistress. You will not disrespect her."

However, his comment was all the more offensive that the exact same shameful thoughts had crossed my mind the first time I had laid eyes on her.

"I mean no disrespect, Clan Leader," Zoltar said in the most insincere apologetic tone. "But she is shockingly fragile to this much pain from such a light flick of the somitan branch."

"Do not be so haughty, cousin," I said in a harsh tone. "Yes, her species lacks the natural protection granted by our scales, but that is no bragging right. We didn't *earn* our genetics. We merely inherited them. She had the courage to uproot herself from her homeworld and come live among complete strangers, bigger, and stronger than she is, plus she's making every effort to embrace our foreign culture."

"Bah," Zoltar said, waving a dismissive hand. "We are a peaceful people. Our customs do not require much sacrifice to adapt to."

"You know not what you speak of," I said, disdainfully. "You mock her, but if you were the one marrying a human female, would you have worn the multi-layered clothes their males wear, with shoes? Would you have kissed your wife when asked?"

"Kissed?" Zoltar asked, the same curiosity reflected on Luped's face and that of the other people listening in on our conversation.

"It is a human custom where they press their mouths against each other's as a sign of affection," I explained.

Zoltar made a disgusted expression. "I would do none of that nonsense. Andturians do not wear clothes or touch mouths with others."

I tilted my head to the side, giving him a scornful look. "So, you would disrespect your mate? You would spit on her customs?"

Zoltar had the decency of looking embarrassed. Once again, he'd shown his propensity to talk first, think later. But that reminded me that Susan had in fact spared me the discomfort of wearing those strange clothes human males wore and would have also spared me the awkwardness of kissing had I not insisted. She was going out of her way to accommodate me.

"You wouldn't dress to honor your mate, and yet Susan made a great sacrifice by undressing for the ceremony," Luped interjected. "Her people do not just cover themselves to protect their soft skin, it is considered offensive to undress in public."

"Why?" Zoltar asked, echoing the question burning my tongue. "Are they ashamed of their appearance?"

"Not at all," Luped replied with a sliver of annoyance at this less than subtle attempt at a barb. "Susan undressed to honor our ways and to please Olix. She only covered what her customs deem otherwise highly inappropriate. She says her body is only for her mate's eyes. Showing her reproductive parts to any other male would be a great disrespect to Olix."

That took me by surprise, but it also greatly flattered me. Others looked intrigued, while Zoltar also appeared confused. Susan returning with my mother put an end to the conversation. She was wearing a long, flowy white dress without sleeves. I wondered if this was the human wedding dress she would have worn had we performed a full human ceremony instead of the basic one she settled for. Still, it made me look at her with new eyes.

It hugged the curves of her chest and torso, a second layer of semi-transparent, highly ornate fabric decorating it. The long skirt, much wider, swished as it undulated with each of her steps. She had kept the ceremonial paint and head fur decorations my mother and sister had put on her. The overall effect was rather pleasing to the eye.

Susan came straight to me, a timid smile on her lips.

"Your dress is quite beautiful," I said, genuinely appreciating the craftsmanship, but also wanting to make her more at ease.

Her face turned red again, throwing me for a loop. I had meant to compliment her, not embarrass her. Further adding to my confusion, instead of the look of humiliation I'd expected to accompany her skin coloration, Susan gave me a broad smile, showing her blunt white teeth, her brown eyes lighting up with pleasure. Did human skin also redden when they were happy?

"Thank you, Olix," Susan said with genuine happiness. "I'm glad you like it."

"I do," I replied, returning her smile. "Come, let us feast."

"Okay," she said in a breathy voice.

We headed to the main table, my mother to my left and Luped to my Susan's right side. We remained standing.

"Thank you, clanmates, neighbors, friends, and family for joining my mate and me on this special day," I said. "I would extend to you the hospitality of Monkoo, but it is we who benefit from your generosity in preparing this bonding feast. Eat, drink, dance, and let us celebrate not only this union, but the enduring friendships of the Andturian clans."

The people tapped their tails and whistled in response. The Gatherers began serving the food, bringing large plates of everything to each table so people could pick and choose what they wanted to eat. Ours was served first. To my delight, Susan didn't act skittish about any of it. She tasted everything, asking questions, especially about the vegetables, but the meats as well. Luped was all too happy to answer her.

Although she enjoyed the berry cider, Susan further pleased me with the restraint she displayed once she realized the strength of its alcohol level. She continued to parsimoniously sip on it, not letting it get to her head.

When the meal ended, the Gatherers—aided by some of my clanmates—took away the remaining food to the kitchen at the back. There, it would be equally divided among the clans. In the meantime, Hunters removed the spits and covered the cooking pits to turn the central area into a dance floor. First, the males and females of each clan performed ritual hunting dances for my mate. The way her eyes sparkled and the enthusiasm she showed in clapping her hands as she observed them earned Susan the approval of the people.

Then, we joined them on the floor. Although she possessed a good sense of rhythm, my mate struggled with reproducing some of our traditional steps. It made me realize how much crouching it involved and the level of lower body strength it required. The absence of a tail to counterbalance some of the movements also increased the difficulty for her to imitate us. But she eventually settled in a comfortable middle-ground that made the steps easier for her while being close enough to the real thing.

One by one, the visiting clans began to leave, those located the farthest leaving first. But the festivities continued well after the sun began to set and long after Susan and I had retired to our dwelling.

CHAPTER 6
OLIX

As soon as the door closed behind us, dampening most of the sound of the ongoing celebrations, Susan's joyous mood faded, and she immediately looked intimidated. An awkward silence settled between us. I wanted the carefree and talkative Susan from the feast back. As much as I liked hunting prey, I didn't enjoy my mate looking at me like she was one.

"I… I should go take a shower and wash off all this paint," Susan said.

Normally, as mates, we would shower together. I almost said as much. But Susan clearly needed some time alone, maybe to gather herself.

"Very well," I said, repressing a frown.

Her nervousness around me bothered me greatly. Still, the grateful relief she expressed upon hearing my answer convinced me I had made the right choice by indulging her request. My female grabbed her bag, still sitting on the communal table and headed straight to the hygiene room. I almost offered to teach her how to use it, but I could only presume Mother or Luped had already shown her.

I headed for our nest chamber while removing the adornments on me. The glowstones in the room lit as soon as they detected my presence. I placed the adornments in their respective casings on the upper shelves near the door, then cast a glance at the room. It was smaller now that Luped had taken up a significant amount of space to build a 'wad-robe' for Susan.

Kayog had stated my mate would need such a space to store her clothes and footwear. As one of our best Builders, my sister had done high quality work in no time. However, it seemed too big to me. Luped insisted that she had performed research confirming some humans would deem it too small as it wasn't a walk-in. She suggested we modify the divisions of the house, and maybe add an extension, so we could build Susan a proper walk-in attached to the hygiene room.

I would ask my female in the morning.

In the morning as well, I would do what I hadn't had time to do in the past two days since the Temern announced Susan's impending arrival, and learn everything I could about humans.

I looked at the sleeping nest, hoping she would find it adequate. We didn't rest in beds, but a large recess in the floor of a more or less circular shape—although some preferred a square one—filled with a large down feather cushion at the bottom and smaller cushions covering the edges. A thick nirka fur lay partially folded at the base of the nest. We used it to keep us warm during colder nights. A set of thin sheets of fabric called blankets and a pair of cushions called pillows that Kayog had sent covered the bottom cushion—that humans would call a mattress.

I didn't see how such light covers could keep humans warmer than a nirka fur, but the Temern insisted that humans required their blankets. If Susan truly liked them, the Crafters would be happy to weave more for her.

To my surprise, I heard my mate coming out of the hygiene room in less than fifteen minutes. I had expected her to hide there a long time, while working up the courage to face me. The rules of the unions arranged through the Prime Mating Agency stated that the couple must be legally married according to both of their species' customs that first day, and that their bond was to be consummated that same night. Failing to do so could result in the annulment of the union and severe financial penalties for the couple since the PMA shouldered all the expenses in getting the partners together. While I understood their need to ensure the mates were serious in making a success of their journey, it also placed a tremendous amount of pressure on us.

And even more so on the male to perform.

Having a few days to get to know Susan before moving to that step would have been nice. Technically, the Temern wouldn't know if neither one of us revealed the truth. For a second, I even considered proposing to Susan that we wait a bit. However, I dismissed that thought. Not only did I not want to risk the penalty, I especially didn't want my mate thinking I was avoiding my duty to her. I'd failed her enough for one day.

But what if she wishes I did offer?

Susan entering the nest chamber, looking just as intimidated, put an end to my musings. The short, translucent black dress she wore couldn't offer any kind of protection. I could see every curve of her body underneath it—or would have if not for the bag she was clutching to her chest as if her life depended on it. Her long head fur was cascading down her back and over her shoulders. It curled in far more accentuated spirals than before the ceremony, now that she had removed the metal wires binding them in thick strands. It made it appear shorter, but it still looked pretty around her face.

"I have finished," Susan said in a timid voice.

I didn't know how to respond to such an obvious statement.

"I will go wash as well," I said, not knowing what to do with myself, before remembering the 'wad-robe.' I pointed at it. "This is all for you to put away your clothes and personal belongings. Feel free to use the space however you see fit."

Her eyes lit up, some of the tension bleeding from her shoulders.

"Thank you," Susan replied.

I grunted in response, then made my way to the hygiene room. Of all the terrible things the Invaders had done to our people during the time they had enslaved us, commodities such as showers, hygienic toilets, and power stones had been a blessing. A part of me wondered how Susan would have reacted had I not been able to provide her with such basic comforts.

But the Vaengi were the last thing I wanted to be thinking about right now. After showering, I dried my scales using a fluffy towel before hanging it next to the one Susan had used. My stomach knotted as I slowly walked back to our nest chamber. I opened the door and found my mate standing next to the shelves of the 'wad-robe' where she had already hung her clothes. As soon as she saw me, she stopped brushing her head fur. Looking self-conscious, she made as if to pull the fur that had remained stuck on the brush but changed her mind. Instead, she placed the tool on one of the shelves and closed the door.

She wrapped her arms around herself, as if to hide her body, which the translucent outfit failed to cover. The extremely short skirt didn't even reach the middle of her thighs. This time, no underwear covered the parts only reserved for my eyes. Despite the folds of her skirt, the exposed slit of her sex was visible. Through the flimsy dark fabric, I could see the round circles surrounding her two tiny teats in the center of the globe-like swells of her chest. What could possibly be the purpose of such a useless garment?

Susan cleared her throat, looking more nervous than ever.

"So... hmm... considering our earlier miscommunications, I was thinking we should discuss this next part to make sure we're on the same page," Susan said with a nervous laughter.

"That is a good idea," I said, both relieved and grateful for her easing us into the topic.

Susan appeared to relax a little, and she smiled in response.

"Maybe we can sit in the bed?" she asked, gesturing at the nest.

"Very well," I said, letting her lead the way.

My mate circled around the left side of the sleeping nest, which sat right in front of a large window. She removed her flat footwear and descended into the nest, sitting at the edge with her legs crossed beneath her. I settled on the opposite side from her, kneeling on the cushion before sitting on my haunches and curling my tail to the side.

"I tried to read up on Andturians mating rituals, but couldn't find a whole lot," Susan said with that same nervous laughter, redness creeping up her neck and cheeks. "I know we are compatible, but just not how your people go about it."

I frowned, unsure what she was really asking.

"Well, the female usually leans against a wall or over a low surface like a table. More rarely, she will get on her hands and knees. She lifts her tail and parts her veil to expose her slit, then the male positions himself behind and penetrates her with his stem," I said, as if it was self-evident—which it should be. "The male pumps into her until she is pleasured, then he releases his seed."

The way Susan stared at me with round eyes, her lips parted in shock, I couldn't decide if she truly hadn't known how people mated or if our ways disturbed her.

"You mostly have sex standing up and from behind?" she asked, stunned.

I blinked, taken aback by that strange question. "Yes."

"Wow, okay. Hmmm… But what do you do before you penetrate a female?" she asked.

The hope in her voice further increased my confusion. Susan needed to hear something from me to reassure her about our mating ritual, but I had no clue what it could be.

"Well, we ask the female if she consents to the coupling. If she's agreeable, she assumes the position, and we penetrate her," I said.

Judging by her dismayed expression, that was *not* the response she had wanted to hear.

"That's it? You guys go from yes to immediate penetration?" she insisted with disbelief.

"Yes," I said, getting slightly annoyed. "What else would there be?"

"Well, foreplay," she replied as if it was obvious. "Have you never heard of foreplay?" she asked when I tilted my head with a questioning look.

I shook my head. "No. What is that?"

"It's... Damn, how do I describe that?" Susan whispered to herself, her eyes flicking from side to side as she pondered. "It's pleasant and affectionate things a human couple does to each other to help the male get hard and the female get wet to make penetration easier."

Wet? What a strange term for lubrication, but appropriate enough, I guess.

My eyes widened as I stared at her in shock. "You need help getting lubricated? Human females do not self-lubricate at will?"

Susan snorted and shook her head. "No, we don't. We need to be stimulated and aroused by our partner to be ready. I mean, we can technically prepare ourselves," she amended, her face reddening again, "but it's more effective when done well by our partner. Some females can't get natural lubrication at all."

Spirits, why is everything so complicated with humans?

I stared at her, starting to feel overwhelmed again. How was I supposed to stimulate her? At the same time, it was nice of their females not to expect a male to be hard on demand but be willing to help him get there. That was undeniably intriguing.

"And how do you do four play?" I asked carefully.

The redness of her cheeks cranked up another notch.

"We caress each other's bodies... and kiss," Susan said in a small voice. "And our couplings are normally face to face, while lying in bed. Not standing up, and rarely from behind."

I almost laughed at the sheepish way in which she had pronounced the word 'kiss.' I had not been too keen about this kissing thing the first time. But the feel of her mouth against mine had been unexpectedly pleasant. I didn't mind doing it again. In fact, I'd been wondering when I'd have the opportunity to test it further. I welcomed this experiment. However, I couldn't help wondering why it was called *four* play when she only mentioned two things.

"I can do that," I said, relieved it wasn't anything more bizarre. Coupling face to face happens sometimes among my people, although quite rarely. "Do you wish to start now?"

"Uh, just a minute," she said, a sliver of panic entering her voice. "There's... there's something else we need to discuss."

I slightly recoiled, wondering what else there could be.

"I'm listening," I replied.

"There's something you need to know about human females, so that you do not panic later," Susan said.

That immediately set all of my senses on alert. Something had to be pretty bad for her to assume I would panic.

"The very first time a human female has sex with a man, there is a good chance that she will bleed a little," Susan said.

"WHAT?! Bleed?" I exclaimed, panic indeed setting in. "Why would you bleed?"

"It's okay! It's okay!" she said, raising her palms in an appeasing gesture. "We have this thin veil of flesh inside. It's like a seal that usually breaches the first time we have penetrative sex. The veil—called a hymen—will tear, which causes a bit of bleeding. But it's normal and stops right away. The tear will sting a little, but no more. Mind you, not every woman reaches adulthood with their hymen intact, even without sex. Various physical activities, even just sports, could cause it to tear. But I still have mine."

I looked at her in horror. I was already worried about lying with a female as tiny and fragile as she. Now, I was finding out that no matter how much care I handled her with, she would bleed the minute I joined with her.

I do not like this, AT ALL.

"It's going to be all right, I promise," Susan insisted when I continued eyeing her with dismay.

Beyond the fact that she would be bleeding, something else troubled me quite a bit.

"Why has no male breached your 'high man' yet?" I asked, unable to hide the suspicion in my voice. "You *are* a mature female of mating age, right?"

Susan gaped at me for a few seconds before bursting out laughing. "Yes, Olix. I assure you that I am a fully mature adult," she said with a smile in her voice. "Legally, humans are deemed old enough to 'choose' to mate as of the age of sixteen. I will be twenty-five years in a couple of months."

That only made my brows furrow deeper, which appeared to confuse her.

"That means, you were able to couple for the past nine years," I said. "Why haven't you?"

I hadn't meant for my tone to come out as accusatory as it did, but too many questions were firing in my mind. Was my female defective? Did the males of her colony not deem her worthy of their attention that none would have attempted to pursue her? Had her temperament driven potential partners away?

She recoiled, her eyes widening at my reaction. "You know, on my homeworld, males would rejoice to find out I was untouched."

It was my turn to recoil.

"In case Kayog didn't tell you, Meterion used to have a religious colony classification," Susan explained while tucking a few locks of her head fur behind her right ear. "The same way we don't show our bodies in public, my people didn't allow others to touch them intimately unless they were married. Back then, there were severe consequences, especially for women. Still having a hymen was the easiest way to prove whether or not they had 'sinned' whereas men don't bleed their first time."

"You are punished for coupling even though you can legally do so?" I exclaimed, shocked.

Susan laughed. "Thankfully, not anymore. Today, we can sleep with anyone we wish, even if we are not married. However, we avoid it, mostly because of the risk of pregnancy," she explained. "Birth control is frowned upon by our people. But land is everything on Meterion. If you let the wrong man impregnate you, the land will move to his bloodline instead of the one you might have wanted."

"But Kayog said you needed to leave Meterion because you didn't have land," I challenged.

She nodded. "As a third daughter, I don't have land or any real hope of making a good marriage on my homeworld," she said with a sigh. "Because of that, pregnancy wouldn't really be an issue as far as land was concerned. Many men asked me to have sex with them, but I refused them all."

"Why?" I asked, surprised.

"I didn't deem any of them good enough for me," she said, lifting her chin defiantly. "On Meterion, it is considered a great honor to be the first man to lie with a woman. None of them deserved it from me," she added, scrunching her face.

"And you deem *me* deserving of it?" I asked, stunned.

"Of course! Otherwise, I wouldn't have married you," she replied matter-of-factly.

That gave me an oddly warm feeling in my chest. "You honor me, my mate," I said, humbled.

She smiled timidly.

"Anything else, I should be aware of?" I asked, bracing for it.

"No… Well… not really," she said, hesitantly.

What now?

I narrowed my eyes at her, and she squirmed on the cushion.

"Well, it's just that since this will be my first time, I am pretty tight down there," she said sheepishly, her face coloring again. It was ridiculous just how easily she reddened. "So, you will have to go slow and be careful depending on how big you are."

The worried look she cast towards my groin would have been comical if not for her genuine concern.

"I don't know what a human would consider big but, by my people's standards, I am well-endowed," I said, carefully. "You fear you won't be able to take me?"

"Oh no! No, I'm pretty sure I will be able to… We stretch and adjust. It just might take longer and be a bit more uncomfortable until then," she said, although I couldn't say if she was trying to reassure me or herself. "But there's no point borrowing trouble. We'll cross that bridge when we get there."

I scratched the scales on my nape, feeling somewhat distraught. This was the most awkward mating night I could have ever imagined. Right now, I just wanted to gulp down a full jug of berry cider and go to sleep.

"Very well," I said, swallowing back a sigh. "Do you wish to begin this four play now, or is there something else to be addressed."

"No, nothing else. We… we can begin if you wish," she said in a thin voice.

I waved my hand over the white stone near the edge of the nest to shade the window so daylight wouldn't bother us at sunrise. I turned back towards Susan whose chest was heaving, her breathing becoming labored from what I presumed to be a mix of fear and anticipation. But the first order of business was to rid her of that useless dress that only highlighted her nakedness rather than cover it.

I advanced closer, walking on my knees on the fluffy cushion and stopped right in front of her. Moving with slow, non-threatening movements, I carefully placed my hands on her lap, right at the hem of her dress, and slipped them underneath to gently lift it up. She didn't balk, lifting her arms to make it easier for me to get rid of it. I discarded the dress at the edge of the nest. The way Susan clasped her hands in front of her, I suspected she in fact wanted to cover her breasts and slit.

My gaze roamed over the strange texture of her scaleless body. Her skin was so pale, smooth, and flawless, I would have compared it to ivory if not for its slight golden tinge. I leaned forward and pressed my lips to hers. She responded in kind. It was as pleasant as I remembered. Except with that done, I'd exhausted my playbook—I didn't know what else to do. I'd never felt so incompetent and clumsy. As I couldn't stay indefinitely with my mouth pressed against hers, I straightened and looked at her apologetically.

"I'm sorry, but I do not know how to please you," I confessed, my scales darkening with humiliation at my failure. "Will you show me what you would like from me?"

The disdainful and disappointed look I had expected from her never came. For some odd reason, my cluelessness appeared to please my mate. I couldn't quite figure out why. Maybe it made her feel like we were on a more equal footing and that, despite my experience, I might as well have been a virgin. Whatever the reason, I was glad to give her the lead—something I'd never expected myself to do when coupling.

"Sure, I can try to do that," Susan said with a nervous smile. "Lie down on your back, please."

I complied, lying down in the center of the nest. Susan prowled closer to me on all fours. There was something oddly enticing in her doing that. Her gaze roamed over me with a curiosity filled with awe. Although I wouldn't have called it desire, the possessive anticipation burning within her brown eyes sparked a pleasant warmth inside me.

Her palms settled on the thick skin covering my abdominal muscles and chest, roaming slowly in a gentle caress. It was pleasant. The soft heat of her hands stirred the first embers of arousal deep within me. She leaned forward and started kissing my stomach without stopping to caress me. Her mouth on my body felt strange and tickled a bit, but I took mental notes of all that she was doing so that I could reciprocate after.

I gasped and slightly stiffened when her tongue began to trace the grooves between my abdominal muscles. Susan paused, her head jerking up to look at me with worry.

"You licked my stomach," I blurted out, stating the obvious.

"Humans do that," she said cautiously. "Is that unpleasant for you? If so, I'll stop."

"No, don't stop," I replied instinctively, surprising myself. But, taking a second to think about it, I realized that her tongue on me had resonated nicely in my groin. "It was unexpected, but quite agreeable."

My mate's shoulders relaxed, and her relieved smile reminded me that she was an inexperienced female. I needed to be extra careful in my feedback to her not to severely undermine her confidence regarding intimacy going forward.

Susan continued tracing the lines of my muscles with her tongue, stopping only a short moment to tickle my navel that way, before moving up my chest. At the same time, she climbed on top of me, her knees settling on each side of my waist. She resumed kissing my body, now focusing on my neck, the curtain of her head fur cascading over my torso provided a silky caress of its own that was quite enjoyable. Tilting my head back to give Susan better access to my neck, I placed my palms on her rounded behind.

Spirits! She was so soft! Instead of the rough scales scraping my palms that I was used to, my hands felt as if they were rubbing over the most expensive Geruvian velvet. Susan shivered when my hands roamed up her just-as-silky back in a slow movement. She rubbed her face in the crook of my neck then her blunt teeth nipped at my scales there, sending a bolt of pleasure between my thighs. I nearly extruded. To think I had feared my female wouldn't arouse me! I could get used to this four play thing.

I purred in approval and tightened my embrace around my female. Susan immediately responded by biting me again and gently scraping at my scales with her blunt claws. I purred again, involuntarily. But it gave my mate the reinforcement needed to know her actions were pleasurable to me. With a will of their own, my hands went onto a more thorough exploration of her body.

But she was straying from her demonstration to me and starting to focus on my enjoyment of our encounter. Moving up to my face, Susan alternated between kisses and nips along my jawline before pressing her lips to mine.

This time, I took over.

She slightly gasped when I turned us around, laying her on her back before reciprocating. Careful not to crush her, I leaned partially on my side and started where she left off by pressing my mouth against hers. She wrapped her arms around me, her delicate fingers caressing my quills at the back of my head. A lovely sigh escaped her as I let my mouth roam over her face, while my hand did the same on her body.

I could already tell that the feel of her beneath my palm would become an addiction of mine. Like Susan had done for me, I paid attention to her responses as I touched and kissed her to understand what she liked. When my lips settled on her neck, it became quickly apparent that her crook and nape were particularly sensitive. Andturians loved to bite and to be bitten. It had turned me on so much when she'd done it to me. However, I didn't dare reciprocate with her skin being so fragile. At least, her breasts also seemed to enjoy my attentions. The way her teats hardened under my palms fascinated me.

As much as I had found the round breasts strange, their cushiony softness made me want to squeeze and play with them endlessly. The way she arched her back to press her breast further against my face when I kissed it didn't go unnoticed. Drawing from her playbook, I timidly poked my tongue out to lick at her teat. Licking one's partner was the strangest thing to do, but the approving moan Susan rewarded me with spurred me on.

I went all out, swirling my tongue over her left teat and the pink circle surrounding it while my hand played with the other. The sound of her heartbeat increasing alongside with her breathing confirmed I was finally doing right by my female. But I couldn't linger there indefinitely. While my mouth shifted its attention to her other breast, my hand traveled further down over her flat stomach. It quivered beneath my touch, and Susan appeared to tense when it moved past her navel.

Lifting my head, I locked gazes with my mate. Her lips parted, her brown eyes looking almost black, she stared at me not with fear but an anxious anticipation that alleviated my concerns. A delicate scent wafted to me, immediately setting my loins on fire. Despite Susan being of a different species, the musk of her arousal was unmistakable. Without looking away from her, I pursued my journey south, my hand settling over her exposed slit.

Susan's breath hitched as I slowly rubbed her before my fingers parted the folds of her slit. Her breathing accelerated, and she opened her legs to ease my exploration. A triumphant growl rose from my throat at finding her slick with her natural lubrication. She could use a bit more, but my four play on her was paying off.

Despite the similarities with our females, Susan's opening differed greatly. Aside from the scale veil naturally covering Andturian females' slits, a thin layer of scales sheeted their inner walls. It scraped against the scales of a male's stem, enhancing the sensations for both partners. But my Susan was as soft outside as she was inside. Or at least, the short distance I could reach in. The thin sheet of skin called 'high man' she had spoken of could be felt about two centimeters past the entrance. The main difference was the warm wetness within. Our females also didn't have a little nub above their slit. Whatever this was called, its sensitivity clearly procured my mate a great deal of pleasure. When she lifted her hips, as if seeking more friction, I started rubbing my fingers over it.

"Yes," Susan whispered in a shaky voice, before closing her eyes.

That hit me like a punch in the gut, and pressure built in my groin as my stem began to throb with the need to extrude and claim my female. Susan shivered and moaned as I accelerated the movement and pressure of my fingers on her. The scent of her arousal grew exponentially, and her lubrication flowed steadily. Although I now believed her ready to receive me, I couldn't stop looking at her face, tense with pleasure.

Susan didn't match an Andturian definition of beauty. Her features were strange to me and would probably continue to be for a while. And yet, right now, as she was trembling and moaning with pleasure under my touch, my mate was mesmerizing to me. She suddenly cried out, her body seizing, startling me. I'd been so entranced that I hadn't realized she was peaking.

I continued massaging her nub until she appeared to come down from her climax. The body of a human female was turning out to be a wonder. Our species didn't have those sensitive pleasure points and didn't require four play. Coupling was a straightforward matter, concluded in a few minutes, with each partner finding their release swiftly. Although this was a much more complicated affair, it was also proving to be a pleasant one, nonetheless.

"Do you require me to pursue the four play?" I asked, my stem aching to be released from its confines.

Susan chuckled and shook her head with a tender expression in her eyes that I liked very much. I almost climbed on top of her, then hesitated, the unpleasant memory of the blood she would spill coming back to the fore. I took one of the blankets and folded it twice before laying it down on the main cushion. Some tension creeped back into my mate. I mentally kicked myself for not having done that first. Still, she smiled timidly once I finished and lay down on top without me having to say anything.

She spread her legs. I barely repressed a sigh of relief as I extruded while settling between them. My eyes flicked towards Susan when I heard her soft gasp. The scared—if not horrified—look she was casting on my stem almost made me deflate. Did it repulse her?

"You're big," she whispered, worry audible in her voice.

Oh! Right...

"Too big?" I asked, carefully.

Susan licked her lips nervously and eyed my stem as if it was some sort of vicious monster that had crawled from under the nest to savage her while she slept.

"No," she said in a small voice that lacked conviction.

"You must be honest with me, Susan," I said in a stern voice. "Is my stem too big? Will it harm you?"

She took in a deep breath and forced herself to look me in the eye. "No, it will not harm me if you are careful and patient," she said in a determined voice. "It will hurt because you are big and I'm tight, but not too much if you go slow. Each time we will do it, it will get easier because my body will adjust to you."

I held her gaze a moment longer to make sure she wasn't just saying that out of a misplaced sense of pride or duty. But she didn't flinch or waver, gesturing instead for me to proceed. Reassured, I complied, surprised my stem was still erect. Susan spread her legs wider, her arms wrapping around my back. For some odd reason, I stunned myself by lowering my head and kissing her lips. She smiled then closed her eyes as I began pushing myself inside of her.

The head of my stem barely made it past her entrance before meeting resistance. My female had been right saying it would take patience. I pressed myself in carefully, my gaze never straying from her face to make sure I wasn't harming her. After another push, Susan cringed a little, and the metallic scent of blood stung my nose. I immediately tried to pull away, but she held me.

"It's okay, I'm fine," she said in a reassuring voice.

Although she looked like she meant it, I could feel the warm liquid around my stem. This felt like *a lot* of blood. I freed myself of her embrace and sat on my haunch to stare at her opening. She started closing her legs, her face turning red with embarrassment, but my hands on her knees stopped her.

"Olix, it's fine!" she insisted, looking mortified.

"It's a lot of blood, Susan," I argued, worried.

"No, it's a normal amount," she said, sitting up. "See? It already stopped. Please, don't ruin this."

That last comment struck a nerve. I didn't want to ruin her first time, but I had a duty to take care of and protect her.

"Do I look in pain to you?" she insisted.

I shook my head.

"I would not lie to you about this. Have you already forgotten how loud I scream when I'm hurt?" she said in a voice that was both pleading, but also attempting to be humorous.

I smiled, tension fading out of my back.

"Yes, my mate. I do," I conceded, still struggling to silence the panicked voice at the back of my head. "Very well. But let me clean you first," I said, using the blanket I had previously folded to carefully wipe the blood off her.

Although visibly embarrassed by it, Susan didn't argue and allowed me to do so. She had spoken true. The bleeding had stopped and there wasn't that much blood after all. However, as I looked at the stained fabric, it struck me that I was looking at the honor my female had bestowed upon me, the only male she had deemed worthy.

"Lie still, my Susan. I will return shortly," I said, rising to my feet before walking out of the nest chamber.

CHAPTER 7
SUSAN

I stared at Olix's receding back in disbelief as he walked out of the room with the soiled blanket. Where the fuck was he going? He was his people's top Hunter, the Spear of the Andturian clans. Surely the smell of blood wasn't turning him off? This whole mess had started so awkwardly, finally gotten great, and was now going down the toilet at neck breaking speed.

I hadn't expected much out of my wedding night, certainly not to be enjoying intimacy with a lizardman, and least of all for him to get me off like a rocket after he'd shown so much cluelessness. But his willingness to learn and to let me show him what pleased me had deeply touched me.

I liked that it had provided me with the excuse to explore his body in a way I wouldn't have dared otherwise. Best of all, he'd seemed to enjoy some of the ways I touched him. I also especially loved that, once he'd gotten the gist of it, he'd taken over and applied what I'd shown him. However, he hadn't simply copied me, he'd actually paid attention to my responses and reacted accordingly.

Olix appeared to be an attentive and generous lover. With time, my husband and I could have a very healthy and enjoyable sex life—and even life in general. But not if he took off on me right in the middle of the deed.

I strained my ear to catch any sound that could reveal what he was up to. Not knowing what to do with myself, I contemplated putting my negligee back on, not that it had seemed to impress or entice him in any way. Since he had asked me to stay still until he returned, I reluctantly complied. As much as I disliked a bully or bossy person, I did like a take-charge kind of a man.

The door suddenly reopening startled me. Although it had felt like forever, Olix had barely been gone a couple of minutes. My annoyance instantly faded the minute I saw him approach the massive, circular bed. The muted lights from the glowstones that illuminated the room played on the green scales of my husband, giving them an almost dreamy aura as I watched his defined muscles ripple with each of his steps. The memory of the feel of them beneath my palm rekindled the flame that his fear about my virginal blood had somewhat doused.

I forced myself not to stare at his still extruded and still fully erect shaft. Olix was seriously well endowed. I may not have had penetrative sex with anyone, but I've had some heavy petting with the couple of men I had considered having a serious relationship with before realizing they just wanted a side piece. My husband had them beyond beat in the girth and length department.

And size wasn't the only difference. While the general shape was comparable, the top length of his shaft had some sort of a hump that was bound to give some extra sensations, and his entire penis was covered in a layer of soft scales. They reminded me of the ones that covered the thick, dreadlock-like strands at the back of their heads that they called quills. A strange name considering they were very pliable and felt more like soft leather strands.

As Olix stepped down into the bed, my inner walls clenched

in both fear and anticipation. It had hurt a little when he had first started inserting himself. But it had been mild, thanks to the care he had displayed, despite my stupid body fighting him. I hadn't even felt the breach of my hymen. In truth, while a part of me was relieved not to have sex while bathing in my own blood, the other wished he hadn't cleaned me up and hadn't stopped. My blood would have served as additional lubricant and, by now, he would be fully sheathed.

Without a word, he settled over me again, although his eyes locked with mine sought to validate that he still had my consent. I spread my legs and wrapped my arms around him in response. He kissed my lips like he had done previously before starting to push himself inside of me. I loved that kissing was becoming a reflex for him or that he was at least making a conscious effort to do it. He'd seemed so turned off the first time. But I loved kissing.

It burned again as he slowly made his way inside of me. Thankfully, he appeared to produce a natural lubricant of his own that was easing him in. I tried to ignore the discomfort between my thighs and focused instead on his lips and tongue on my neck. The small scales around his lips gently scraping my skin resonated directly in my core. To my major relief, although narrower and longer than a human's, Olix's tongue wasn't forked. For some reason, that would have freaked me out. And its rougher texture felt amazing against my skin, and especially the way it had teased my nipples. Right now, it was doing wonders on the particularly sensitive spot in my neck.

I was half-sighing, half-moaning with pleasure when my body suddenly gave up the fight and yielded. Olix went from halfway in to fully sheathed. That burned and drew a startled yelp out of me. My husband froze, his head jerking up as he looked at me with worry.

I smiled reassuringly. "You're in," I whispered. "Good job."

He relaxed slightly, but not fully. "Are you all right?"

"Yes," I said with a nod. "You've done really well."

This time, he fully relaxed and smiled, the most adorable mix of relief and pride descending on his alien features. To my pleasant surprise, he didn't start moving right away. I didn't know if Andturian females also needed a moment to adjust to their male's girth, but Olix waited, covering my face and neck with kisses. Only when, with a will of their own, my inner walls began contracting around him did my husband start moving inside me.

Holy fuck! I had feared the scales of his shaft would wreck the soft lining of my inner walls, but I couldn't have been more wrong. It was the most exquisite sensation, overtaking the underlying discomfort of feeling so incredibly stretched and full. And that hump on the top length of his member? Did I ever feel it! It seemed to undulate almost like a wave, massaging an incredibly sensitive spot inside me with each stroke.

The uninterrupted series of moans flowing out of my mouth were quickly joined by the growling ones from Olix. One look at his face completely messed me up. My man had stopped kissing me. Eyes closed, teeth clenched, his features constricted as if under extreme pain, Olix appeared to be fighting not to lose control due to excessive pleasure. I could feel him pick up the pace, taking me deeper and harder, only to emit a frustrated grunt and rein himself in.

A part of me wanted him to throw all caution to the wind and let his passion run wild, and the other feared he would destroy me. Still, in no time, he was vigorously thrusting into me, head thrown back while emitting that sibilant hiss mixed with a rattling sound that had creeped me the heck out at the spaceport. This time, it was sexy as fuck.

My skin felt feverish as liquid fire ran through my veins. My entire body began to shake with my impending climax. Then Olix called out my name followed by a series of words in his native language. I didn't know what he had said, not that it mattered. But the almost feral passion with which he said it sent me over the edge.

I shouted as violent spasms took over me. My erratic movement impeded Olix's possession of me. He slipped an arm under my right leg, lifting it, opening me wider to him and restraining some of my shaking. And then he went to town on me. I couldn't say whether he had fully lost control or simply given in a bit more, but he pounded into me with wild abandon. Although it hurt a little, the pleasure of his scales and hump were driving me to the brink of insanity. I never fully came down from my first climax before he wrested another from me, this time, joining his voice to mine.

Olix slammed himself home, and his seed shot out violently inside of me. It was surprisingly hot, not so much it burned, but enough to notice. He didn't move, although a series of spasms shook him while he continued to fill me with short spurts of his essence. When he finally appeared to reconnect with reality, he looked at me, shock descending on his features as if he was just now remembering he'd been brutally plowing into me.

"Did I hurt you?" he asked, almost panicked.

"Are you kidding? That was amazing!"

His jaw dropped and, for a second, he stared at me as if he wanted to make sure he'd heard right. When I beamed at him, the pride and joy that descended over his features turned me upside down. I realized then that, like me, he hadn't expected much good to come out of this night.

"I am glad I was able to satisfy you, Susan," he said in a deep, grumbling voice filled with emotion. "I have never experienced this much pleasure with a female. You are a wonder, my mate."

Okay, now *that* messed me up big time. I didn't even know what to say, not that I could have spoken a word my throat was so constricted. But Olix didn't appear to expect an answer. His shaft still buried deep inside of me, he turned us over. Lying on top of him, I felt incredibly vulnerable and yet completely protected. He extended a hand towards the big fur at the edge of the bed and while pulling it over us, his tail flicked over a blue stone embedded in the floor next to another pair of colored stones by the bed. All the lights turned off.

Purring with contentment, I rested my head on my husband's chest while the heat of the fur settled over me, and his tail wrapped around my legs. I didn't fully know what the future held for us, but after our rough start, I was starting to believe we would make it.

I woke up feeling wonderful—although a little sore south of the border—the divine mattress and cushions around me feeling like a nest of clouds. To my great disappointment, Olix had already left. It shouldn't have surprised me though. There was a six-hour difference between my native region on my homeworld and Monkoo Valley. I would therefore be jetlagged for a few days before adjusting to this new time. The shading still active on the window made it hard to know the current time.

Wading through the cushions, I reached for the stones embedded on the floor by the bed and waved my hand over the white one, lifting the shading on the window. It revealed the beautiful flower garden and green area between our house and the neighbor's. The brightness outside surprised me. By the looks of things, it was probably close to noon.

Groaning inwardly, I crawled out of bed, quickly tried to give it a semblance of order, then donned a robe before exiting the room. While unsurprising, I was further disappointed not to find Olix in the living area. On the table, a nice breakfast had been left for me consisting of crunchy, slightly sweet cereal-like grains with nuts and fruits, and a thick smoothie-like drink. Even though there was probably more than I could eat, from what I had read about the Andturians, this was a somewhat humble portion, especially since it didn't include any meat. And yet, my gut told me they had been generous with me.

Kayog's words about the situation of the Andturians kept replaying in my mind. Olix's short speech when thanking the other clans for their generous contribution to the feast further reinforced my belief that I could be of great help... if they let me.

I quickly showered, loving the stone design that created the illusion of a waterfall. The toilet was a different story, though. From what I'd seen so far, my new people didn't possess a single seat with a backrest—ditto with the toilet. It was merely a cylindrical stone seat, hollow in the middle, in a corner of the room. With the damn thing being slightly wider than a human toilet— the hole as well—I had to be extra careful sitting at the edge not to fall in. I felt like a child transitioning to grown-up toilets after completing my potty training.

At first, I had wondered at the lack of backrest everywhere, then I remembered their tails. During the banquet, I had noticed that all of them either tucked it under their benches if they were standing on legs, or curled it around the base to avoid people inadvertently trampling or stepping on them. I would have to sweet talk someone into making me a special chair that I could lean back in to relax.

When I walked out of the house, the village was bustling with activity. The large plaza, where my wedding had been held last night, appeared to have been transformed into an outdoors workshop. Males and females were all working in a relaxed atmosphere, crafting a variety of magnificent objects, from jewelry to housewares and weapons. At the far back, a couple of forges had been set up. Zoltar was currently working at one of them, while Olix stood nearby, talking with a few other males. I didn't know whether to make my way over there or leave him be for now.

Yamir—my mother-in-law—spared me from further pondering by abandoning whatever task she was doing and coming my way as soon as she saw me. Her broad grin and the pride displayed on her face instantly put me at ease. Last night had been such a rollercoaster of hits and misses that I had not quite known what to expect this morning.

"How are you feeling, Daughter?" Yamir asked as she came to a stop in front of me, her golden lizard eyes giving me an assessing look.

"I feel great, thank you. And after such a wonderful feast last night, I had not expected to be able to eat anything, but that breakfast was so good I devoured it all," I said with a smile.

Although Yamir smiled, a sliver of worry flashed through her eyes. "I'm glad you enjoyed it. Was it too little? Do you still hunger?"

"Oh no!" I exclaimed, shaking my head. "It was more than enough. In truth, it was a bit too much. I do not have a very big appetite."

Yamir's shoulders relaxed. That drove me to prod a little further, hoping not to offend her.

"I understand that the food situation has been getting a little challenging in the region of late," I said carefully. "Is that true?"

She nodded, her face taking on a serious expression. "Hunters have been having a difficult time finding game in their usual hunting grounds. Something is causing a migration of the herds. They have to travel farther now and compete with other predators in those new areas. The situation isn't dire," she added quickly as if fearing her words had frightened me. "There is enough for everyone to eat. We're not starving. Olix will be leading another great hunt in a week."

I nodded and smiled to show I wasn't concerned at all. "During the feast last night, there were many delicious side dishes with various roots and vegetables," I said nonchalantly. "Where did those come from?"

"Our Gatherers harvest some of them in the forest and by the river. The rest, we trade for with other species in the monthly public market," she replied.

That piqued my interest. "The public market?" I asked.

Yamir nodded. "The first day of every month, a large outdoor market is held outside the spaceport. All the native species bring the various goods they have to offer for sale. The majority of the customers come from the tourist resorts that have been built on our homeworld over the past few decades, as well as a couple of new communities that we have allowed to settle on our planet after their own was decimated by natural disasters. The main refugees are the Bosengi. They are very wealthy and have this silly propensity for flaunting their wealth by acquiring expensive things that can help further display their status."

Despite the obvious criticism in her voice, Yamir didn't express disdain but more amusement in the face of a behavior she clearly considered as silly. However, this interesting tidbit of information had not fallen on deaf ears. I would dig further into that public market business.

I cast an assessing glance at the Andturian working on the plaza, my wheels spinning.

"Should I presume then that all the crafting ongoing right now aims at preparing goods for the next market?" I asked.

"Yes," Yamir said, puffing out her chest with pride. "We are crafting the finest items for convenient use around the dwelling, elegant adornments for the body, and exquisite weapons, both for hunting purposes and to be used in ceremonial settings. Not only do we use unique and highly resistant materials, but we also craft them honoring centuries old techniques and traditions."

I bit the insides of my cheeks not to smile. You'd think she was doing a sales pitch. She didn't have to convince me, but I could relate to this kind of passion about a craft passed down from generation to generation and that you devoted your own life perfecting.

"That's wonderful," I replied with sincerity. "I hope to learn more about it in the future and maybe even try it out myself."

"We will be happy to teach you," Yamir said with approval.

"Do you ever sell or trade some of the food harvested by the Gatherers?" I asked.

She looked at me as if I'd suddenly grown a second head. "Absolutely not," she said firmly. "We have to be careful in our harvesting not to deplete the area too quickly. Therefore, our vegetable consumption is controlled. With the scarcity of game lately, we have overexploited the natural resources of the forest. We could not afford to sell or trade these precious resources."

I licked my lips nervously, grateful for this opening onto the subject had been itching to broach ever since my arrival here.

"Yes, that is sensible. However, although I haven't had a chance to have a close look at them, you appear to have vast lands behind and around the village," I said nonchalantly. "Have you ever considered growing that produce there instead? That way you'd have plenty to eat and to sell or trade with?"

Yamir recoiled and gave me a shocked look as if I'd said something highly offensive.

"Absolutely not! We are Hunters, not Farmers," she exclaimed, her voice dripping with disdain. "Surely you wouldn't suggest turning my people into dirt diggers?"

I stiffened, feeling deeply offended by her words.

"First, I'm not trying to turn anyone into anything," I replied with a slightly clipped tone. "Second, what's wrong with being a farmer? You do know that I am from Meterion, one of the major farming colonies of the solar system, right?"

She pinched her lips and had the decency of looking some-what embarrassed, realizing how offensive her words had been to me. "There's nothing wrong with your people doing what they do," Yamir said coolly. "But *our* people are Hunters, and my son is the greatest among them."

"Fair enough," I said, swallowing back the urge to snap at

her. "But what's the point of hunting if there are no animals to hunt? Hunting is a gamble. Farming, when done well, is pretty much a guarantee. Considering the difficult times our people are facing, don't you want to contemplate options that could make sure we won't starve?"

The savage expression that descended on my mother-in-law's face twisted my insides. Her green scales taking on a pinkish—not to say reddish—hue was all the warning needed to know I better retreat immediately before I pushed her too far.

"You will *not* put crazy ideas into my son's mind, do you hear me?" she hissed with such venom it took all of my willpower not to run for the hills. She took one menacing step towards me. "Olix is facing enough challenges right now without you making him look weak. Once before, off-worlders nearly destroyed our people by turning us into dirt diggers. You will not enslave us again."

On these harsh words, Yamir turned around and stomped back to the small table she had been working at amidst the others. Every single pair of eyes was locked on me, curiosity and worry shining within in equal measure. A female whose name I didn't know asked Yamir a question as soon as she sat down. By the annoyed, dismissive gesture my mother-in-law performed, I could only guess the female had inquired about what had just happened, and that Yamir had refused to answer. No wonder, if she felt this strongly that my hint about the people farming could so severely undermine Olix's standing.

The challenge I faced was going to be far greater than I had anticipated.

CHAPTER 8
OLIX

The glow of pride I felt preening under the envious stares of the others as they gazed upon the trophy Susan had bestowed upon me faded at the sight of my mother's anger. She had been so happy when she first went to greet my mate. What could have possibly transpired through their conversation to cause her to be so upset her scales would redden?

I excused myself and headed directly towards my female who seemed both embarrassed and distressed. She watched me approach with a mix of relief and guilt.

"Good day, my mate," I said, stopping in front of her. "Are you well? Is everything all right?" I asked before casting a sideways glance at my mother.

Susan shifted uneasily on her feet and chewed on her bottom lip while thinking of her answer.

"I'm fine," she said carefully. "I guess I asked a question that your mother did not appreciate. I didn't realize it was that sensitive of a topic. I didn't mean to upset—"

Susan froze, her eyes widening as she gazed upon the leather harness adorning me. I puffed out my chest, making the harness stand out even more. Her eyes flicked to my wristbands and then to the hilt of the hunting knife hanging on my hip. I had woken at dawn and labored all morning on this.

"Is... is that blood?" Susan asked with an air of disbelief.

"Yes!" I said proudly. "Your gift to me."

Her jaw dropped, but I couldn't decide if horror or wonder prompted that expression.

"I have cut the sheets only to keep the bloody parts and treated them with tormedium," I explained with enthusiasm. "It has darkened or burned out all the fabric that didn't have blood on it so the blood would stand out. Then I have divided it into perfect sized pieces for my harness, wristbands, and weapons. You only see the dagger now, but I also have a part of you on my hunting lance and bow," I added with a grin. "Then I covered the pieces in purified sotomac resin to seal them forever in this current state and then embedded each piece in the various accessories. I sewed them in the leather myself and did the blacksmithing as well. There is one last piece however that I have requested one of the Crafters to set for me," I confessed sheepishly. "My touch isn't delicate enough to craft jewelry, and I want two strands of your blood as ornaments for my quills."

Susan continued to stare at me for a moment longer, apparently rendered speechless by what I had done.

"Wow," she finally whispered in a tone that I couldn't interpret. "You went through all this trouble to wear my virgin blood?"

"Of course! You have chosen me above all others to share your first and only blood. It is a great honor that I do cherish," I said with sincerity. "I get to carry this special piece of you with me, everywhere I go. The other males are dying with envy. No other among our people will ever receive so unique a gift from his mate."

A flurry of emotions fleeted over her features. Susan snorted then shook her head as if she couldn't believe it before giving me a strange smile.

"You are very sweet, Olix. I am glad it pleases you," Susan said in a soft voice.

She smiled and caressed my upper arm affectionately. The gesture reminded me of her touch on me last night, the softness of her around me, her moans in my ears. I clamped down on the thoughts as my stem threatened to harden again. Now wasn't the time to couple with her. I just hoped she would wish to repeat it tonight.

However, looking at my female, it was plain to see she didn't understand why I had done this with the bloodied sheets and probably found it bizarre. A part of me was disappointed my work hadn't elicited the proud and joyful reaction I had anticipated. However, even though she didn't quite understand it, my reasons for doing it had touched her. In the end, that mattered the most.

I smiled back before movement at the edge of my vision reminded me of our original topic of discussion.

"But, going back to your conversation with my mother, what question did you ask that upset her so much?" I asked carefully.

Susan looked troubled again. "We were talking about the public market and the fact that your people are crafting items for sale. I asked if you've ever considered using all the lands you have at the back to grow produce to sell at the market."

My spine stiffened, and I barely reined in my own anger wanting to come to the fore.

"Judging by your reaction, it is definitely not the question to ask," Susan said with a sad expression.

That made my anger melt. I didn't want to upset my female. It was a fair question to ask, especially considering her background. That was but another thing I should have taken into account when informing Kayog of my requisites for a mate. Then again, had I excluded farming, Susan wouldn't be by my side right this instant, and she was rather growing on me.

I sighed and nodded. "Let me give you a tour of the village

and surrounding areas, and we can talk at the same time," I said, gesturing towards one of the paved paths. She smiled and fell in step with me. "Farming is a sensitive topic for my people ever since the Vaengi upended our lives. Five generations ago, they came to Xecania. It was my people's first contact with an alien species. As we've lived in harmony for centuries with the handful of other species inhabiting our planet, my ancestors had no reason to expect treachery from these newcomers."

"But they enslaved you instead," Susan said.

I nodded. "Their first action, before they even spoke a single word, was to kill the Clan Leader," I said in anger. "Everyone else was given a collar that inflicted pain and could even cause death if they refused to obey. For the next 54 years, my ancestors were forced to work the land until they died of exhaustion. The Vaengi called it farming, but it was a desecration of the land. The earth and water were poisoned by the chemicals they forced my people to use. It caused terrible rashes to those who worked the fields. Some of their scales even fell off and never grew back."

Susan covered her mouth in horror as she listened to the tale, barely looking at the various houses we were walking past.

"My people suffered horribly. We would probably still be facing that same hardship if not for one of the Vaengi savagely beating a young female named Molzeg," I continued.

Susan gasped. "Molzeg? As in the elder that married us last night?"

I smiled. "Molzeg and Pawis—our Elder Gatherer—are the only two still alive who had interacted with the Vaengi as they were both younglings at the time. Everyone else you see here was born after our ancestors routed them. When the adults started tending her wounds, they noticed her collar had been damaged from the beating."

"Wow," Susan whispered, her eyes widening in awe. "I bet your people were panicking at the thought the Vaengi might discover it and replace it with a functional one."

"Yes. That was exactly their fear. They would never have another chance like this," I said, pleased that my mate was so caught up in the story. I gestured at the Great Hall that we were just passing in front of. "This used to be the common room shared by all my ancestors under slavery. They slept, ate, and lived there the few hours they weren't working the fields. Molzeg was lying inside that day, being treated. She was a willful child, barely eight years old, and demanded they all heal her as best they could then went back to the fields."

"Right there and then?" Susan asked, impressed.

I nodded. "She walked past one of the supervisors isolated from the others and jumped on him. Even as children, Andturians possess greater physical strength than the Vaengi. She had no difficulty overpowering him, despite her wounds. His controlling device failed to cause her pain. So, she killed him, took the device, and used it to release the others." I looked at my woman with a triumphantly vicious grin. "They massacred the invaders who took too long to realize the collars no longer worked. They had grown so complacent that they didn't have the original lightning weapons they had used to subdue my people."

"You killed them all?" Susan asked, her eyes sparkling with a vengeful glee that pleased me tremendously.

"Some of them managed to flee," I said, shaking my head. "The next day, they returned with greater numbers, but my people were ready. They had spent the night recovering all the Vaengi's weapons in the dwellings and practicing using them. They hid in the nearby forests, some in the fields, and only a handful in and around the buildings then basically hunted down the invaders. My people moved faster, were stronger, and knew well how to hunt. The Vaengi's technology did not save them."

"So, after another defeat, they finally let you be?" Susan asked.

"Not right away. They came back a couple of times and failed both attempts. We had their technology to warn us of their approach. They failed because they assumed we were too stupid and primitive to understand," I said with disdain. "But what truly convinced them to leave was that our Hunters went to the other species inhabiting our world to also find them enslaved. They freed them using the devices and helped them slaughter the invaders. The Vaengi realized there would be no easy way for them to reclaim what they had lost."

"So, how did the United Planets Organization manage to get a foothold here and convince you to join their alliance?" Susan asked.

I laughed. "It took quite a few attempts from them, and a lot of near tragedies for the emissaries they sent. But it was the Temerns that convinced us to speak with them. Like Molzeg, they have affinities to see beyond what others can. They understood our emotions and how to interact with us in a way that would build trust."

"Their empathic abilities," Susan said with a nod.

I smiled in agreement. My mate sighed, a somewhat disappointed expression descending on her features.

"And ever since, your people have been dead set against anything revolving around farming," Susan said with resignation. "I knew your people had been enslaved, but now I understand better why you feel so strongly against working the lands again."

"I am pleased that you understand," I said with relief while continuing the tour of the village.

I pointed out the various points of interest, including the larder, the dry food storage areas, the location of crafting materials and equipment, as well as those of completed arts and crafts. We didn't have a store or currencies per se within the village. Anything we wanted, we traded for in exchange for another item or service. In some cases, a request would simply be granted in exchange for future compensation. Nonetheless, whenever someone no longer wanted or needed something that was not expected to be sold at the market, it was placed in a common storage. Anyone who wanted it could simply take it. Otherwise, every dwelling had an individual storage for things we wanted to keep and not give away.

Susan expressed a great deal of interest in the common storage. While I had no issue with her redecorating our dwelling however she saw fit, the things that held her interest confused me. Still, I continued the tour, showing her the school, meditation gardens, healer's hall, play areas for the children and the different ones for the adult sports and physical activities, and then the pier and beach area.

But just as I was readying to conclude the tour, Susan insisted on visiting the land surrounding the village. I immediately got a bad feeling about that request. Nonetheless, I complied and showed her what she wanted. The awed expression on her face as she walked over the abandoned field further distressed me.

She crouched down at one point and took a fistful of soil, breaking it between her fingers before letting it trickle back down to the ground. It had taken years for the environmental damage of the Vaengi's farming methods to be reversed. Some of it was due to the United Planets Organization sending experts to clean the toxins in the land and water.

Although Susan said nothing, I could see her wheels turning and the excitement growing on her face. She then noticed a couple of abandoned buildings at the edge of one of the largest fields behind the Great Hall.

"What is that?" she asked, pointing at it.

"The one on the left used to be a tool shed, while the one on the right used to contain seeds and other farming resources," I explained.

"Can we take a look inside?" Susan asked in a voice full of hope.

I stared at my female for a second, my discomfort increasing exponentially. Agreeing with a stiff nod, I led her to the buildings. During the whole walk there, her eyes flicked in every direction as she took in the environment. As far as I knew, it didn't differ much from the human's original homeworld, planet Earth, aside from our more colorful vegetation and our three moons. In their world, most plants came simply in various shades of green, and trees mostly had brown bark. On Xecania, the leaves on the majority of the plants were purplish blue or a brownish red, although we did have plenty of greenery, too. And our bark tended to be in darker shades without ever fully being black.

The buildings both sat unlocked. Despite the many years of disuse, like everything in Monkoo, they'd been built to last. A bit of dusting and airing would suffice to make them usable again as their former contents had been disposed of decades ago. The spark in Susan's eyes as she explored the large buildings further twisted my insides. I stood still by the entrance of the former shed, bracing for what would follow.

"Any chance I could make use of these buildings?" Susan asked.

"Just the buildings?" I asked, already knowing the answer.

She shifted on her feet and rubbed her nape with a guilty expression on her face.

"Well, I'd also love to be able to use part of the land outside," she admitted in a sheepish voice.

I stared at her, forcing myself to silence the anger bubbling below the surface. I didn't want my scales to turn red on my female, especially not the day after our union. But Spirits! Had she not heard a word of the story I'd just told her? She'd acted as if she understood how my people felt after our liberation, and not even an hour later, she was asking me for land?

"Look, I can guess what thoughts are going through your mind right now," Susan said in an appeasing tone. "I understand what tragedy befell your people, and that you have all since forsaken farming. I respect that. I'm not asking you or any Andturian to work the land."

Although I remained circumspect, those words alleviated part of the tension stiffening my spine.

"However, *I* am a farmer. My entire life has revolved around working the land. It's what makes me happy," she said carefully. "These lands are the richest and most amazing I have ever seen in my entire life. As a third daughter, I have never owned land. I only got to work those that belonged to others. This… this would be my chance to finally have a little something that's mine. But it would also allow me to have a bit of home with me."

Her words, and especially the longing in her voice, troubled me.

"How would it allow you to have a bit of your home with you?" I asked, confused.

"Last night, the feast was wonderful," she said in a gentle voice. "But as much as I enjoyed every dish, all of them were completely foreign to me, not only the recipes, but the ingredients used. From my conversations with Luped, Xecania doesn't possess any of the produce that are the foundation of human diet. Can the Gatherers find me potatoes, squash, or portobello mushrooms in your forests? There also are no strawberries, corn, or garlic here. How would you feel if you moved to a world where you would never again be able to eat roasted jovam roots?"

I recoiled at the horrendous thought. Jovam roots were at the heart of the Andturian food culture. Jovam was used in everything. Boiled, roasted, mashed, fried, it could even be turned into dessert.

"I would go insane if I were to never have it again," I conceded.

"Well, this is currently what will happen to me," Susan said, the pleading tone seeping back into her voice. "I am condemned to never again eat my version of jovam, unless you allow me to use a part of your lands to grow some human produce that cannot be found here. And we both know how prohibitive the cost would be if I tried to have some transported here from another planet just for me."

I nodded slowly. She would never find a transporter who would go through such trouble just for her, not to mention the complication of transporting perishable items over a long journey in space, and the risk of introducing contaminants in our ecosystem.

"All right," I said carefully. "But why do you need both buildings?"

"My personal belongings will arrive later today or tomorrow," Susan explained, getting excited again. "I own very few things that aren't farming related. I only have some clothes, and everything else are things I had hoped to use to grow some human produce. Mostly equipment and seeds for the things I've described to you. I would use part of the shed to store that equipment, and the other part to grow mushrooms. They do quite well indoors."

That would actually help reduce complaints from the people. The less they saw her farm outside, the better it would be.

"And the other building?" I asked.

"It would be for my seedlings," Susan said. "I will plant the seeds in small containers and start growing things indoors for the first two to three weeks. It is better for some vegetables to be started off that way before being exposed outside. These buildings have huge windows, so there will be plenty of sun coming in, without the problem of bugs, wind, or possibly excessive rain."

That, too, would be good. Two to three weeks to give the people more time to get to know her and make their peace with her needs might help things go over more easily.

"How much land would you need?" I asked.

All the tension that had bled out of me came back with a vengeance upon seeing the look on her face.

"All of that area," she said, showing a massive section of land with her index finger.

"WHAT?!" I exclaimed, feeling both offended and like I'd been played for a fool. "You said you just wanted a small section to grow things for yourself!"

"I DO! I promise, I do!" Susan said, raising her palms in an appeasing gesture. "I know it looks big, but it's not when you think of it. I want to grow multiple things: potatoes, squash, watermelon, cabbage, lettuce, tomatoes, cucumbers, beans, corn, and wheat, just to name a few. For each of them, I need a certain area for multiple of those plants to grow. That adds up."

"Why do you need multiple if it's only for you?" I insisted.

"Because vegetables take time to grow," my mate explained patiently. "Some take weeks, but most take months. If I only have one or two plants of everything, I'll only be able to eat certain things for two days every three to four months and have nothing left in-between. That's terrible! But if I have multiple plants, I'll be able to eat some every week."

Once again, it was a fair point. And yet, my gut told me that I was being conned. Nevertheless, I found myself forced to accede to her request for lack of strong counterargument.

"Very well, Susan," I said, making no effort to hide my reluctance. "You may use both buildings and the parcel of land you requested. "BUT you will be discreet about your activities and not try to lure others into working the land. If you need help bringing things here, or having specific tools crafted, you may ask for assistance, but do not be surprised if few consent. It is nothing personal. However, you are opening a very sensitive wound for my people. I hope you understand that."

Susan appeared troubled by that comment. While it saddened me to dampen her enthusiasm, I appreciated that she seemed to grasp the seriousness of the matter.

"I promise, I will not flaunt it," she said, sounding chastened.

"I swear that I am not trying to cause trouble for you, and I do not wish to disrespect your people in any way."

Somewhat mollified, I grumbled a response then herded her back to the plaza. But even as we were approaching it, the silhouette of a transport shuttle in the distance announced the arrival of Susan's personal belongings. As worried as her farming plans made me, her squeal of delight and the joy on her alien face made it impossible not to smile as well. Her happiness pleased me.

Luped joined forces with me to unload an impressive number of crates and containers onto a hover platform while my mate raced back to the shed to start cleaning it. By the time we were done moving all of her belongings into the two buildings, the sun was already setting on the horizon. Despite her eagerness to start sorting out and organizing her belongings, Susan willingly came back to the Great Hall with us for the evening meal and community gathering.

There would be time enough for her projects on the morrow.

CHAPTER 9
SUSAN

L ast night, although no one gave me the stink eye, my new people didn't show me as much warmth as during the wedding celebration or the morning after. News traveled quickly in a small village. Yamir hadn't shared the subject of our conversation that had stirred her anger—which still lingered—but unloading my farming equipment had given me away.

My poor Olix had been in damage-control mode all evening. I never would have guessed how deep the wounds of the past still ran, even though only two of those who had actually suffered under slavery still lived today.

Try hard as I may, and despite the genuine empathy I felt for their ancestors, I couldn't understand their current reaction, let alone agree with it. How could I? I wasn't in their shoes. I hadn't lived through the fallout of rebuilding their society and sense of self after routing the invaders. Still, as much as I believed they were taking the wrong approach with this specific issue, I had to respect their feelings and not try to force my will or views onto them.

I no longer thought it possible to achieve Kayog's dream of turning the Andturian into farmers like my people on Meterion.

There was still a sliver of hope they would change their minds, maybe once they saw the success of my own crops, but I wouldn't hold my breath.

Nonetheless, after Olix explained to them how refusing me would equate to someone depriving them of ever eating jovam roots again, the people suddenly showed a bit more empathy towards me. Yamir remained a little stiff, but in the absence of me trying to promote farming, she slightly relaxed. The rest of the evening went on smoothly, concluded by a very hot night with my husband.

Olix was a quick study who seemed to genuinely enjoy fore-play, however clumsy he had been at first—not that I was much more skilled to begin with. Last night, he insisted we shower together. My initial shyness was short-lived. My man's hands were all over me in no time, and I loved how he touched me. I never expected to get so turned on by someone who looked so different, and even less that he would grow this attracted to me. And yet, since our first night, I'd caught Olix stealing heated glances at me throughout the day. During that shower, his desire for me had been undeniable.

In truth, I suspected he'd barely resisted the urge to prop me up against the stone wall and bang me right there and then. I'd wanted him to, but after we dried up and took things to bed—or our sleeping nest as he called it—I was beyond grateful for his restraint. It would take a few more nights of slow and careful penetration for me to adjust to his girth without feeling on the verge of getting split in half. Still, sex last night had been even better than the first night—after the initial awkwardness—and was promising to become epic in the future. I just had to work up the courage of bringing up oral sex...

But for now, kinky thoughts needed to take a backseat. I'd once again slept in this morning, although not as late as yester-day. Olix had already been up and about for a while by the time I emerged from the house. After greeting the people all busy crafting on the plaza—including my mother-in-law who seemed a bit warmer today—I made a beeline for my shed to unpack my treasures. I had to make haste as I wouldn't be able to work tomorrow.

I'd found out that, although they followed a 7-day week and 12-month calendar, the Andturians didn't have a traditional 5-day work week. Adults worked and children studied for two days in a row, rested one day, and worked two more days, rinse-repeat. Saturdays and Sundays held no special meaning to them. Every day was either a work day or a play day, with the rare holiday marking special moments of their history—like their liberation from the Vaengi, Summer Solstice, or the Day of the Spirits.

After my conversation with Olix, I had spent the evening pondering how I would go about things. Unpacking helped me clarify in what order I would proceed. Kayog had mentioned including a gift for me in my belongings. I had not expected the two large bags of germinating mix that I found there. I squealed in delight as I had expected to have to beg for manure and make the kind of rough mix that would never compare to a proper compost mix that would take months to create.

I had wanted to bring some from my homeworld, but it never would have passed customs. Even the seeds that I had brought almost didn't make it. Thankfully, I managed to sweet talk my husband and his sister into bringing in a few tables from the common storage. I would need more stuff, but would try to carefully work my way into getting the assistance I needed without being too pushy.

For now, I wanted to get my seeds started. In a week from now, Olix and most of the Hunters would set off on a hunting expedition that would last at least a couple of weeks. As much as it saddened me, I hoped that by the time he returned, I'd be able to make him sample a few things that might stir his interest into seeing more of what allowing me to work the land could provide.

I picked up my propagator racks from one of the containers. Each rack contained thirty cells that I filled with germinating mix before planting one seed per cell. After covering the seeds with more mix, I lightly watered them then placed a greenhouse cover on top of the rack to keep in the moisture. I repeated the process with a variety of vegetables, from tomatoes to broccoli, cauliflower and kale, cabbage, and squash, and obviously potatoes. I hated that I couldn't start from an actual piece of potato as my original seed, but that would have never passed customs.

I was almost done with my tenth rack when a knock on the door startled me. To my pleasant surprise, Luped was paying me a visit—although I suspected it also involved some snooping.

"Already hard at work, I see," my sister-in-law said, her lizard eyes flicking this way and that.

"No choice if I want to eat some potatoes soon. It will take at least two months from today for them to grow, but three months is more likely," I said with a pitiful face.

She gave me a commiserating look. "At least, you have hope it will come," she said.

"Indeed. I'm pretty excited about it," I replied.

"I see that you've already used up two of the tables we brought," Luped noted.

"Yeah," I said scrunching my face. "Getting the seedlings started quickly is my number one priority. After that, I will go looking in the common storage for something that could act as shelves for my racks so that I can keep the tables closer to the windows for the sprouts that will need a lot of sun. Then, I will need to get hay, straw, or woodchips and find a way to get some really strong hooks on the ceiling of the backroom to grow mushrooms."

"Hooks to grow mushrooms?" Luped asked, surprised.

I nodded. "There are different ways to grow mushrooms, but hanging them in a tube is my preferred method. It also makes it easier to harvest—I find."

Luped pursed her lips, pondering. "I can build the shelves and install the hooks for you," she said. "You just need to give me the measurements and the type of weight you need to hang."

My jaw dropped, and my eyes all but popped out of my head. "Really?" I asked, floored.

Luped nodded. "I am the main Builder and architect of the clan," she explained. "I mainly work with wood and stone, but I have been studying a lot of the foreign techniques involving metal. This will be a nice change from my usual tasks."

I squealed and, without thinking, I hugged Luped and hoisted myself on my tiptoes to kiss her cheek. She froze, looking at me with a stunned expression. I flinched, promptly letting go of her before giving her a sheepish grin.

"Sorry, I got carried away in my enthusiasm," I said, embarrassed.

I could see her wheels spinning, an uneasy expression settling on her face.

"I didn't mean to offend you," I added slightly worried. "It is common for humans to kiss people on the cheeks as a sign of thank you."

Luped slightly recoiled, confusion replacing her discomfort. "Thank you?" she echoed. "I thought a kiss was a sign of affection or love between mates?"

"Oh God!" I exclaimed, understanding dawning on me. "Did you think I was coming on to you?"

Luped's beautiful blue scales darkened with embarrassment, and I couldn't help myself from chuckling some more.

"You are a very beautiful Andturian, but I am not making advances to you," I reassured her. "I am only attracted to males, and I saved myself for my husband, your brother. If all goes well, there will never be another male for me."

Those words pleased Luped tremendously, and she smiled in approval.

"Humans kiss for various reasons. It all depends on where

you kiss," I explained. "Adults only kiss their mate on the lips, but sometimes, they can do it to their very young offspring, too, as a sign of love or affection. With everyone else, it will be the cheeks, which can be as a greeting, as a thank you, or to show affection. It can be the forehead, usually as a sign of tenderness or as a blessing. It can also be on the back of the hand or on the fingers in greeting, but usually as a sign of respect and deference."

"Hmmm, it is a complex system with many nuances," Luped said with a slight frown.

"It is," I said with a nod, wondering what she would say if I told her some kissing involved tongue play.

"I accept your thank you kiss with a warm heart," Luped said. "You are bringing new things, ways of thinking, and craft that could be useful to the people. Change is always frightening. Do not expect much support from the clan. But as long as what you do doesn't undermine my brother, you will have my aid."

My heart skipped a beat upon hearing those words. After her mother's reaction yesterday, I had not expected help from anyone, least of all from her. But this?

"That means a lot to me, Luped," I said, my throat constricted with emotion.

She looked at my seedling equipment and the other crates I had only partially emptied, a slight frown marring her forehead.

"Andturians didn't use to have currency," she explained. "We still don't. Before the arrival of the off-worlders, we used to trade for goods with the other species. We mostly offered decorative items, weapons, and medicine crafted according to our ancestral methods. Our base materials were the bones, horns, fur, and organs of the creatures we fed from and of course, stone, wood, and metal. But everything has changed with the tourist resorts."

"The demand has increased beyond your capacity?" I asked.

"No, it has disappeared," Luped said bitterly. "Their industrial replicas have hurt our business. Why wait for the monthly market and pay full price for our goods when they can get them instantly for cheaper in one of the spaceport or resort stores? The quality they get is terrible, but visually, it is disturbingly similar. And those corporations can build dozens of replicas in the time it takes us to build a single one."

My heart ached for the Andturians. These were common questionable practices whenever galactic corporations managed to set foot on underdeveloped planets.

"There are legal recourses you can take against that. The United Planets Organization has strict rules against such things," I argued.

"Yes, but the complexity of the complaint system is almost impossible to navigate," Luped countered. "And the other native species do not suffer the same way from these practices. Therefore, it makes our case harder to defend."

"I see," I said with a frown, determined to look further into this.

"And now, with animals running scarce, our sales prices have to be even higher, which makes us even less competitive," Luped said. "It is disheartening. I wouldn't care if that simply meant our people going back to being isolated from strangers. But if this keeps on, we will be starving. All the pressure currently rests on my brother's shoulders as the Spear of the Andturians. Every clan looks to him. And the Conglomerate making offers to buy our lands are making matters worse. If the next couple of hunts and public market sales aren't successful, I fear some of the neighboring clans will give in. It will destroy my people."

I felt blood drain from my face. I had known the situation to be difficult, but not this dire.

"Tell me, Susan," Luped said, eyeing me with a strange expression, her head tilted to the side, "why did you come here despite Kayog telling you of our hardships?"

"Honestly, because I knew I could make a difference," I

said matter-of-factly. "You have amazing lands, and I have expert skills in farming. I was thrilled at the prospect of turning the situation around for your people in the space of two-to-three months. But I never expected there to be such fierce push-back. I understand your history, but I don't understand allowing past tragedy to let you starve when such a simple solution exists."

"And now that you know that things are not going to be what you thought?" she insisted.

In that instant, I realized she wasn't asking this lightly. My answer could define the future of our relationship going forward.

"I left my world to come here. I have sworn to be by Olix's side, for better or for worse, until death do us part in both the human wedding ceremony and the Andturian one," I said, holding her gaze unwaveringly. "My word is my bond. I do not know what the future holds, but whatever comes our way, I will face it with him."

Luped's face softened, and the tension that had creeped up in my back faded.

"I do not know if my people will ever embrace what you have to offer, even if they starve to death," Luped said with a frown. "We are pretty much indoctrinated from birth against it, and it's not a natural interest for us. But we must evolve. The rest of the world is moving forward, and we are being left behind. I believe that if we are not careful, we will be driven off our lands and then become extinct. Olix is fighting a difficult battle between honoring our ways and trying to lead us into the future. I also believe that you are a clever female. As long as it won't hurt Olix, I will assist you in any ploy you come up with to help us move forward."

I grinned, my heart soaring at finding this unexpected ally. I extended a hand towards her. Luped stared at it, a little confused. She repeated my gesture, leaving her hand in front of mine. I grabbed hers and shook it.

"You've got yourself a deal," I said with a grin before explaining what shaking on a deal meant.

She shook her head at me, amused. "Now that we are in agreement, please give me the details on what you need built so that I can get started," Luped said. "You also asked for hay, straw, or woodchips. We have hay and woodchips. Do you have a preference?"

"Woodchips would be ideal," I said. "The smaller the better, but I have a shredder if needed. I would need the equivalent of six of these crates."

"Very well," Luped said, giving me a funny look but not arguing.

While she went to fetch the woodchips, I pulled out my datapad and browsed through the specs of shelves and hooks I'd been considering while planning all the things I could grow on Xecania before my departure from my home world.

The woodchips she brought back needed more shredding. They were leftovers from the Crafters, which they used to start the fires in the cooking pit of the Great Hall. I gave her the specs for the shelves and hooks, then shoved a bunch of woodchips in the shredder, leaving it to work its magic while I continued preparing my seedlings.

Luped came back a short while later with a hovering platform ladened with wooden planks and tools, immediately going to work on the shelves outside the shed I was using as a greenhouse. Watching her lift those huge planks like they weighed nothing blew my mind. But more importantly, although I mostly considered myself a loner, seeing her working 'with me' through the large windows was a major boost to my shaken enthusiasm. I didn't feel so unwanted.

By the time she finished building the first set of shelves, I was done with all my seedling and shredding. Sadly, tomorrow was a play day, so she would build my hooks the day after, and then make more shelves. Before calling it a night, I used one of the fire stones—a polished stone similar to the glowstones that lit our house but that could heat like a hot plate—to boil some water. I filled a few empty containers with the shredded wood chips and poured the boiling water over them to let them pasteurize overnight.

When we rejoined the rest of the clan for evening meal, the curious and speculating looks of the Andturians failed to retain my attention. The dark and hungry gaze of my mate had me throbbing in all the right places and wondering what the heck had him so triggered.

CHAPTER 10
OLIX

With the great hunt coming next week, I had a lot of preparation and coordination to do. All five Andturian clans would be heading out together to cover a greater area. We rarely used technology, preferring to stick with our traditional tracking methods. However, this hunt was far too important. The situation of Clan Leader Surtas was becoming critical. They had been the first to be hit by the scarcity of game. And now, their Gatherers were finding less and less to harvest in their woods. We four other clans had spared what we could, but with our own reserves running low, another failed hunt and public market could force his hand into selling his lands.

This would be a fatal blow to our people as all the hunting grounds and lands surrounding the Inosh Mountains would be lost to us. I refused to entertain that possibility.

Using the map software had allowed me to get a better overview of the location and direction in which the herds were moving based on the latest sightings by our scouts. I hoped that planning things this way would bless us with better results.

As soon as I completed that task, and with an hour left before the evening meal, I decided to seize this opportunity—for the rare times I fiddled with a computer tablet—to consult the knowledge database to which the United Planets Organization had given us access. Since the arrival of the tourist resorts and the Bosengi refugees, the knowledge network had significantly expanded, not only with accessible information, but also with real-time features from tracking, online ordering, communicating, etc.

Over the past few years, Luped had made increasing use of it while mostly failing at convincing me to do the same. However, we had all witnessed how much it had benefited her. The practical things she had learned through it had significantly enhanced her building skills, taught her how to make clever furniture, additions, or modifications to existing ones, showed her ingenious dwelling designs, and above all how to maintain and improve our current dwellings. They had been built decades ago according to Vaengi specs. Over the years, that technology—from plumbing to heating, and everything else in between—had become dated and some of it even obsolete. Without Luped and her research, many of the comforts we had come to take for granted would have been lost.

Yes, we needed to learn more and not be left behind by all the other species, both on Xecania and off world.

But it wasn't new technology that held my interest right now. I had started reading more about humans, kicking myself for not having found the time before Susan's arrival. It would have made the first day so much less awkward. Although my mate and I communicated well, I believed she was keeping a number of things from me. I couldn't say if it was out of embarrassment, because she didn't think I would understand or want it, or because she wasn't interested in it. I suspected the truth lay somewhere in-between the first two options. The way she looked at my lips whenever we kissed only reinforced that sentiment.

I performed a search for human coupling. The first results were extremely boring documents that focused more on the human anatomy and the physiological aspects of mating. I knew the mechanics. I just wanted to know better how to please my Susan.

I modified the search to look for human coupling rituals. That was slightly better, although a lot of it focused on courting a female, and then a series of pretty useless things to 'set the mood' before mating. Apparently, you should feed your mate first—although most of the meals suggested appeared to be desserts or small, unfulfilling treats. The other recommendations included: playing meditation or sleep-inducing music, dimming the light in the room to make seeing difficult—only to semi-fix it with a bunch of candles, and littering the floor or sleeping nest with flower petals. Why did they need the mood set, anyway? You either wanted to couple or not. Even now, just thinking about my female had my stem torturing me with need.

Then I searched for human coupling videos—it would take me days to recover from the trauma.

The variety ranged from highly educational to downright horrifying. It took me a while to differentiate which knowledge sites had the horrifying ones and which had the educational ones. Although even the latter had categories that disturbed me.

The first thing I learned was that humans used their tongues for far more than licking the grooves of a male's abdominal muscles or the teats of a female. Why would that species ever think that licking inside the mouth of another made sense? And yet, every single video had extensive displays of it. The couples also licked and sucked each other's genitals. How did that make sense? Human females even swallowed their mate's seed—which prompted me to search if a human female could be impregnated that way. They could not. So, why did they do it?

The males and females it was done to sure seemed to enjoy it.

And that made me question my reluctance. After all, kissing had seemed gross to me at first, and now I enjoyed it. But did I really want to consider Susan and I licking each other's tongues and genitals? Other things I flat out rejected, like putting my stem in my female's anus, being brutal with her like the males were with their partners in some of the videos, urinating on her, and other actions so disgusting I wished I could wipe them from my memory.

Oddly, the image of a female willingly submitting to being bound by her mate, leaving her helpless to whatever he wished to do to her intrigued me more than I wanted to admit. Picturing Susan at my mercy that way had me throbbing with need. Yes, I would experiment with the humans' strange mating rituals tonight.

Zoltar's voice calling me for evening meal had me guiltily closing all the pages and wondering how to erase my search history. Few people used the computer tablet. Therefore, we only had a handful shared by everyone in the village. Many had already been a little too curious about mating with a human. I'd been deftly dodging their questions. I didn't want my queries to send them down the trail I'd just followed. They might get the wrong idea about Susan.

Until I'd properly deleted it all, I would hang on to this tablet... especially since I wanted to read up more on this Kama-sutra thing I'd discovered right before Zoltar came to fetch me.

I headed to the Great Hall where I found my mate and sister already seated at our table. It pleased me greatly how well they seemed to be getting along. My mother had gone from angry to reserved, but it was only a matter of time before she warmed up to Susan again. Mother was overly protective of me. She wrongly assumed I was fighting hard not to be demoted from my role as Clan Leader because I wanted the power. I was fighting because I didn't want to see our people be exterminated, and because I couldn't think of anyone else who could get this done.

Nothing would have pleased me more than to let someone else shoulder that burden.

Susan's brown eyes locking with mine dispersed the dark

clouds these thoughts had brought out. I loved the way they sparked when she was happy, and the affectionate smile she always bestowed upon me whenever she saw me. My mate didn't love me, nor I her, but a timid friendship and tender bond was blossoming between us. I wanted to further fan that small flame.

As we settled to eat, I caught myself constantly stealing glances at my female. The way she licked her fork after taking a bite of meat completely derailed my brain. The videos I'd watched earlier kept replaying in my mind, all of them featuring Susan and me. My stem ached, and my abdominal muscles kept clenching painfully with need. I wanted to drag her out of the Great Hall and take her straight to our sleeping nest. To my shame, it wasn't for me to do to her what the human males had done to their females, but to feel her mouth around my stem.

The strange looks my people started giving me and the way my mate squirmed on her seat soon made me realize I was making a spectacle of myself. I summoned every bit of my willpower to control my emotions, at least in appearance. After the evening meals, the clan usually remained in the Great Hall to enjoy some music, singing, or dance shows from our gifted members, or to listen to either ancient or newly invented tales by our storytellers. To my relief, it was singing tonight. No one would blink if someone left during any show other than a story-telling evening.

The minute Susan finished her meal, I rose from my seat, caught her hand, and pulled her after me. Although surprised, she didn't resist, her small hand closing around mine the way some of the images on the courting advice page had shown, with couples walking hand in hand. Many gazes followed us, some amused—having no doubt guessed what had me almost going feral—and others curious. My female appeared both excited and worried, as if she suspected the reason for my behavior, but feared she might also have guessed wrong.

As soon as the door of our dwelling closed behind me, I picked up my Susan and headed straight to the hygiene room. Her dress and footwear annoyed me, even though I understood their necessity. The urge to tear the fabric off her rode me hard, but I fought it. I didn't want to scare her and had no idea how much she valued that specific piece of clothing.

My female didn't resist when I hastily stripped her, and thankfully handled by herself the removal of that aggravating breast restraint she called a bra that always challenged me when trying to rid her of it. I had meant for us to be quickly in and out of the shower to explore those other human coupling rituals in our sleeping nest, but my impatience got the best of me. I crushed her lips in a slightly brutal kiss—not as much as in some of the videos, but not as overly carefully as I had done previously. Susan didn't seem to mind and responded in kind.

I fisted her head fur at her nape. No, not head fur. The videos had called it hair. It was so strange how its texture and volume changed when wet. The males had directed and controlled the females using it. Some of them had done so too violently, but in other cases, the females had appeared to enjoy it. I tightened my hold, careful not to harm her, and Susan moaned softly—not in pain—while pressing herself more against me. Emboldened, I parted my lips still pressed against hers and poked my tongue at the seam of her mouth.

My mate recoiled. Her closed eyes snapped open, and she pulled her head back to give me a stunned expression. I tensed waiting to see her reaction. Her eyes flicked between mine, searching, as if trying to assess if she had correctly interpreted what I had done. Had I been wrong about the videos? Some of them, I genuinely believed were perversions Susan wouldn't agree to. But were *all* the videos perversions?

Time appeared to stand still for a moment while we stared at each other, the sound of the water cascading down on us almost deafening in the otherwise silent room. Then Susan gave me a timid smile and rose to her tiptoes to kiss me. I lowered my head to meet her halfway. This time, she parted her lips first, although she didn't poke out her tongue. My heart leapt, and I carefully tickled the opening of her mouth with my tongue, evaluating her response before pushing further. When her arms tightened around me in an encouraging fashion, I decided to take the dive —quite literally.

My tongue slipped inside her mouth, only to be greeted by hers, in a gentle caress. Too many emotions and sensations coursed through me to properly process them. Like everything else about my female, her tongue was soft, not rough like our own. It was almost akin to licking a polished stone, but a warm and pliable one that tasted of berry cider. The odd shape of her tongue, wide at the base and narrower at the tip, made it all the stranger as mine circled around hers.

The interaction was awkward at first, but we quickly adjusted, our movements coordinating. I hadn't quite known what my physiological response to kissing with our tongues would be. I'd mostly expected to be repulsed and disgusted. Instead, it fanned the flame of desire in the pit of my stomach and resonated in my stem.

When I broke the kiss, Susan licked her lips as if she wanted to capture the lingering taste of me and stared at me with sparkling eyes. She had enjoyed this, too. How much would she enjoy me licking her slit? What would she taste like down there? Her skin had been slightly salty when I had licked her teats—no, nipples they called it in the video. Her mouth had tasted sweet, although the berry cider she had drank during evening meal had played a significant part.

My curiosity now ignited wouldn't give me peace until it was sated. Without stopping to kiss and caress her, we washed each other. Discovering that this also constituted appropriate four play greatly pleased me. After thoroughly rinsing the soap from between her thighs so that I would get my mate's true taste, I turned off the water. Susan reached for the towels, but I caught her wrist and pushed her against the wall. Surprised, she gave me an inquisitive look.

Her gaze darkened, and she softly gasped when I pinned both of her wrists above her head with a single hand. The females had seemed to enjoy some level of restraint. The way Susan's breathing and pulse picked up while I kept her thus immobilized and my hand roamed over her appeared to confirm that assessment. The unexpected sense of power it procured me was oddly enticing. I kissed her with my tongue again, my fingers finding their way to her slit and swollen nub. She moaned in my mouth, and I barely kept from extruding. I wanted so badly to lift her up against the wall or turn her around to thrust into her. But Susan was still too tight to take me without careful penetration. Soon enough, that would happen.

For now, I released her wrists with some reluctance and broke the kiss as my lips traced a path down her soft skin, past the hardening nipples of her breasts, over the quivering muscles of her flat stomach, and below her navel. The closer I got to my prize, the stronger the scent of her arousal titillated my nostrils, setting my blood on fire.

Susan's breath hitched when she realized where I was headed. Her lubrication coated my fingers probing her slit when my mouth got closer. Slipping a hand behind her left knee, I lifted her leg over my shoulder. My mate began breathing in quick, shallow breaths, sounding on the verge of hyperventilating from anticipation. I could almost hear the pounding of her heart from where I knelt in front of her. When I carefully licked at her slit, my tongue flicking over her little nub in the process, Susan emitted a strangled cry and fisted my quills.

That sound, the scent of her musk, and the tart taste of her essence on my taste buds had my stem extruding with a will of its own. Fighting the burning need to bury myself deep inside of my female, I tentatively licked at her again.

"Yes," she whispered, in such a needy voice that my stem ached, and my seed boiled inside of me.

I went all out, accelerating the movement of my tongue on her, trying to emulate what the other males had done in the videos, while thrusting my fingers in and out of her. The moans of pleasure interlaced with words of encouragement spurred me on. Although the taste of her essence neither enticed nor repulsed me, her scent in my nose and her reactions to my tongue quickly made this my new addiction. My stem was so hard, it hurt. From the sounds Susan was making and the way her leg on my shoulder shook, she would soon climax. I needed her to fall apart in my mouth, before I could dry her, take her to our nest, and finally find my own release.

As if she'd heard my silent plea, Susan cried out. Her hands held my quills with such strength it stung in a surprisingly delightful way. Her inner walls constricting around my fingers reminded me how they felt, squeezing my stem from all sides in an exquisitely painful way when she climaxed under me.

I pulled my fingers out of her, lowered her leg, and rose to my feet. If not for the wall supporting her, I suspected Susan would have collapsed. The blissful expression on her face filled me with pride. I had failed her in the first day of our union, but I was learning. Picking up a towel, I began to dry her, my mouth claiming hers in the process. She opened for me again, not minding the taste of her own essence on my tongue.

In my impatience, I hastened through drying us—although mostly her—leaving Susan's hair quite damp before carrying her back to our nest. When I laid her down on the main cushion and joined her, my mate didn't lie down but forced me onto my back. Did she want to ride me like some of the females had done in the videos?

My brain froze when, after kissing me with her tongue, my female kissed her way down my body towards my groin. A grunt escaped me when her dainty hands closed around my stem. It was her first time touching me there. Our previous times, I'd always extruded right before penetrating her.

As she prepared to reciprocate, a heavy weight appeared to settle on my chest, constricting my lungs. I couldn't seem to draw enough air in as she stroked me, her lips kissing, nipping, and licking the leathery skin around my pelvic area. My natural lubricant made the motion of her hand on me easier. Although I was too big for her fingers to fully close around me, the way she squeezed my stem while caressing me had a pool of lava bubbling in the pit of my stomach.

And then the wet heat of her tongue teased my tip. Another grunted moan escaped me, my abdominal muscles contracting painfully with need. Leaning on my elbows to look at my female, I realized that, like me with her, she had also wondered what I would taste like. The way her eyes widened and that her lips stretched discreetly, Susan was pleasantly surprised. Relief flooded through me. I had feared she might be repulsed by the taste of my lubricant. What if it had been bitter or acrid? I would have felt both embarrassed and humiliated.

But all coherent thoughts fled my mind the minute my female's mouth closed around my stem. The searing heat of her mouth exceeded that of her slit as she began to bob over me. I was too big and too long for her to take all of me into her mouth —which made me even hungrier to ride her. However, my girth also meant she had to open wide to accommodate me. Despite that, her blunt teeth scraped against the delicate scales of my stem. Combined to the exquisite heat and almost unbearable softness of her tongue rubbing against my length, I cried out with pleasure. My loins ached with the need to release my seed, as my female carefully bobbed over me.

I wanted her to take me in deeper, faster, and for her hand on me to actively work in counterpoint to her mouth on me. But she maintained a slow and steady pace that was pure torture. Unable to resist, I fisted Susan's hair, holding her in place, and began thrusting my hips upward.

Big mistake.

My mate yanked her head back, my hand fisting her hair involuntarily pulling on them in the process. She cringed in pain, one hand flying to the back of her head, the other clutching her throat while she coughed, her eyes watering. The fog of arousal completely dissipated, I sat up in a panic.

"Susan! I'm sorry! Are you hurt?" I asked, rubbing her back, wondering if I should run to fetch the healer.

She let go of her hair and raised her palm in a way that I couldn't decide if it meant to give her a moment or if she was attempting to appease me. Maybe it was both. Neither option reassured me as she coughed for a few more seconds, before swallowing painfully and breathing loudly. I'd never felt so helpless and angrier with myself.

"I'm sorry. I'm so sorry," I repeated, not knowing what to do.

Susan straightened, sat on her haunches, and gave me a shaky smile while wiping her tears with the back of her hands. I felt horrible. Once again, I had made a mess of things.

"It's okay, Olix," she said in a soothing voice before clearing her throat. "No harm done. But you can't do that, or you will choke me. At least, you can't do that for now," she added sheepishly. As her cheeks were already red from nearly choking, I couldn't tell if the color was also due to embarrassment. "Some women can handle it, but I'm not skilled or experienced like that. Well, I'm not experienced at all. This was my first time."

"And I ruined it," I said, hanging my head in shame.

"No! No, it's okay!" Susan said, scooting closer to me. She caressed my quills and looked at me with surprising tenderness when I should be the one comforting her. "I've always wondered what it would be like to have someone do that to me, or for me to do it to my partner. You were amazing in the shower. I didn't think Andturians did that," she added with a nervous laugh. "I was a little scared doing it to you because you're so big and you have this lubricant. But you taste really good, like cotton candy."

"Cotton candy?" I asked, although my scales darkened with pleasure at her compliments despite my failures.

"It's a sweet made with fluffy sugar," she replied with a dismissive gesture before looking at me seriously. "I don't want you feeling bad about intimate things happening between us. You are learning how to mate with a human, and I'm learning everything about sexuality, period. I will be clumsy sometimes, and we will both make mistakes. But this is our journey together. No shame, no guilt, just trust."

I looked at her in awe, a wave of affection blossoming in my heart for the delicate female.

"You are a good and kind mate, Susan," I said, caressing her cheek.

"I think you are a good and kind mate, too, Olix," she replied in a gentle voice. "I like you a lot, and I want our marriage to be very successful and happy. I want us to always feel comfortable telling each other everything and anything, and to be able to make mistakes without fear of being judged or rejected. We are partners for better or for worse. I am your safe haven as you are mine."

"We are," I said with fervor, drawing her into my embrace. "Your species and culture confuse me, but I am glad you chose me. You are opening my eyes to things I never even would have contemplated... like this kissing with our tongues."

She chuckled and then frowned, an inquisitive look descending on her features. "How did you learn about that?"

My scales darkened before I could control them. "I know so little about your kind and how to properly please you, I did some research and watched some videos," I confessed.

Susan's jaw dropped, and she gaped at me disbelievingly. "You watched porn for me?!"

I squirmed and nodded cautiously. "It was a word shown

on many of those sites, yes," I said. "Some of it was distressing."

"No shit!" Susan replied, looking like she couldn't decide whether to be shocked or laugh her head off. "There's some really freaky shit out there that we will absolutely never, *ever* do!"

Relief flooded through me. "I am pleased to hear you say that. It was… distressing."

She laughed. "I can only imagine. I wish I could have seen your face," she added wistfully.

I glared at her, which only made her chuckle again. Then her face softened, and she caressed my cheek affectionately.

"Kidding aside, it really means a lot to me that you would take time from your busy schedule to research how to please me," Susan said. "Maybe… maybe it's best in the future if we watch those videos together? Then I can tell you what is definitely not okay, and what might be fun to do or try."

The timid way in which she asked, like she was suggesting something forbidden made her all the more endearing.

"I would love that, my mate," I said with sincerity. "Maybe I'll have fewer mental scars then."

She burst out laughing and kissed my cheek. Her gaze roamed over me and settled on my partially deflated stem. My blood immediately rushed to my groin.

"Should we give that another try?" Susan asked.

Although she had worded it like a question, I instinctively knew she was making a statement that she wanted to try again. The memory of the warmth of her mouth on me, of the blissful way her blunt teeth scraped my scales, and of her soft hand stroking me had me throbbing again. Yes, I wanted us to try that again… and yet…

"Not now, Susan," I said in a gentle voice.

She slightly recoiled, looking both surprised and confused.

"Despite my earlier impatience, I enjoyed it very much," I

explained. "But right now, I want to lose myself inside of you. I've been thinking about it all day."

Susan licked her lips nervously, her face taking on that expression I'd come to associate with lust, and that did wondrous things to me.

"Okay," she whispered, lying on her back.

I settled between her legs, claiming her mouth with that tongue kissing, and caressing the nub of her slit to make sure she was still sufficiently lubricated to receive me. Then, the divine feeling of her tight walls closing around me had me hissing with pleasure in no time. For the next eternity, our bodies merged in that ancient dance where two became one and time ceased to exist.

She was my safe haven, my home... and I was hers.

CHAPTER 11
SUSAN

The next morning, although still feeling a little jet-lagged, I rose almost at the same time as my husband. Sadly, too late to play naughty again before heading out. I still couldn't believe he had watched porn for me. The thought that we would watch some together and openly explore our sexuality was sinfully thrilling. Such a thought would have been deemed pure debauchery on Meterion.

Although we were still in the very early days of this marriage, things were looking quite promising after appearing hopeless and grim on the first day. The farming drama was a completely different ball game, though. We'd have to see how that would end up down the road. For now, there would be no 'dirt digging' for me as it was play day.

It was a little disorienting coming out of the house and not finding the plaza crowded with Crafters working on their stuff. A few clusters of people chatted away, some clearly making plans. Quite a few were walking out of the Great Hall, having just finished their breakfast. Unlike evening meal, where everyone gathered to eat at the same time, people took breakfast and lunch at varying times, according to their morning routine or tasks during the day.

I walked into the Great Hall, surprised to find large bowls of the cereal they usually ate for breakfast occupying the center of the main table where Olix and I usually sat. Next to them, bowls of fruits, nuts, and bottles of juice were spread out in a way that made it easy for people to self-serve. Olix was filling two bowls with the sweet grains when I walked up to him.

He grinned upon noticing my approach and handed me the smallest bowl, before adding some nuts and fruits in it, then pouring me a glass of that thick smoothie his people made. I loved how he took care of me, and especially how gender equality was a real thing among their people. The fact that males and females possessed an almost identical physical strength no doubt played a role in it. Either way, seeing my man fetching and preparing breakfast for me was beyond sexy.

We joined a group of clanmates eating at one of the round tables inside the Great Hall. While chowing down on our food, we discussed our options for play day. Out in the plaza, two groups were already forming—one would go swimming at the beach, the other would play a ball game that sounded like a weird mix of soccer and basketball, but with multiple baskets. You could only touch the ball with your hands when it turned black. Once it turned yellow, you had better drop it to the floor and stick to kicking it around or your hands would get a very unpleasant sting. The color of the nets also changed, alternating between the team colors. You wanted to make sure you didn't score while it was the wrong color.

Some people would stay right here and play board games inside the Great Hall or outside on the plaza. A few of the artistically driven Andturians would seize this free day to work on new dance choreographies, composing new songs, or writing new stories to be presented after evening meal. Others chose to use that free day either to do things around their houses, to spend a romantic day alone with their partner, or go on a family outing with their spouse and offspring.

Olix and I chose to go with the swimming group. I hadn't been to the beach in forever. As an accomplished swimmer, I couldn't wait to show off my skills. When we finally set off, I realized that a number of the people in our group were also the ones that would be going on the fishing expedition next week.

Many children also accompanied us. They were beyond adorable with their heads that seemed too big for their bodies and their crazy long tails. It fascinated me how they could move about so gracefully without tripping on them. However, I'd also come to realize that their long tails played a major role in keeping their balance, especially with their bigger heads. Their bodies would catch up over time.

As much as Olix wearing my virgin blood as trophies had freaked me out, I couldn't help but be both amused and touched by his grumpy reluctance to remove his accessories when we reached the beach. I removed my dress, folding it before laying it down on a big rock right at the start of the sandy area. The sand was an even darker grey color than the tree trunks of this planet, but still shone as if it had absorbed a constellation of stars.

"This 'sand' used to be normal soil," Olix explained. "But it became contaminated by the pesticides and fertilizers the Vaengi forced my people to use. The soil was literally crystallizing on the fields. After each harvest, the slaves had to shovel layers of dead earth out of the fields and toss them here or in the river."

"Is that why the sand is so dark?" I asked, bewildered by such disregard for the environment and for the plight of the slaves.

Olix nodded. "Yes. It was toxic and killed a lot of the fish, plants, and small animals in the area. We owe the United Planets Organization for cleaning the toxin. But we decided to grind that hard soil into sand and turn this place into a beach."

My eyes widened, feeling both impressed and confused by

such a decision. "Why did your people decide to do that?" I asked.

My husband's gaze roamed over the beach, which extended on close to 500 meters, a glimmer of pride shining in his golden eyes.

"So that we would never forget what had been done to us and to our lands," he said with a fierceness that made me shiver. "This dead earth turned into a stunningly unique beach stands as a reminder that even in our darkest hour, we didn't give up until we prevailed. We turned horror into everlasting beauty, and death into a place where our children play and enjoy their freedom."

"Your people are fighters," I said, my heart constricting as I once more realized what deep wounds the Vaengi had left behind.

"We are," Olix said with a determination that hinted that his mind had now shifted to the new hardship faced by his people. "We didn't give up then, and we won't give up now. But today is play day. This is no time for somber thoughts. Let us see you swim, little human."

My chuckle died in my throat, and my stomach flip-flopped when he gave me a heated once over, noticing at last my sexy burgundy bikini. My mate had a very healthy sexual appetite. If not for all the people around, including the kids, I suspected we would have set the river to boiling with our burning passion.

Olix made that rattling hissing sound that had become an auditory aphrodisiac for me, making my nipples instantly hard and causing moisture to pool between my thighs. His nostrils flared, and a smug smile stretched his lips. The fiend knew how he was affecting me. He leaned forward, his scaly lips brushing against my ear.

"Later," Olix whispered in a deep voice filled with promise.

Feeling weak in the knees, I let him take my hand and lead me to the clearest blue water I'd ever seen. To my surprise, it was freshwater. Then again, I should have guessed since this was in fact an artificial beach.

Most of our group was already frolicking in the waves. My worries to have so many of the little ones swimming around evaporated in a blink. They might as well have been fish. They zipped through the water at incredible speeds before jumping out to make little acrobatics before diving back down. I could have stared at them for hours.

The water was so clear, I could see them swimming underneath, their arms stretched in front, their legs together moving like a mermaid's tail. Sometimes, they would flap their arms to get a boost. They moved with incredible grace.

"How long can you hold your breath?" I asked as we entered the water, surprised by the extensive period of time some of the children remained under.

"We have gills," Olix said, brushing his quills to the side to show a bunch of scales beneath the opening of his ear parting to reveal the gills.

"Oh wow! I'm every shade of jealous right now!" I said, dipping down to my neck into the cool water.

Olix laughed. "Still, we can't stay indefinitely underwater. After more than thirty-minutes, we could drown. We avoid staying under for more than fifteen to twenty minutes."

"I guess I'll have to buy myself one of those organic breathing masks so that I can keep up," I replied teasingly.

"Sounds like a plan," Olix said.

We started swimming, my husband observing me at first to see how I was faring. Once reassured I could hold my own, he began playing with me, literally swimming circles around me. He always looked so grumpy, seeing this playful side of him tickled me pink.

When he realized how much I envied the kids' acrobatics, Olix had me clinging to him, my body as flat along his as possible, so that we could do them together. Granted, we couldn't do anything as crazy as the kids did that way, but it was still insanely thrilling. I held my breath while he raced underwater at dizzying speed before jumping out and trying to remain airborne for as long as possible before we fell back in.

After a few rounds that way, Olix made me remain as straight as possible then, holding my feet, he pushed me forward while swimming hard so that we could gain momentum. At the last minute, I curved upward so that he could propel me out of the water like a cannon shot. Each time, I shot out at least three meters above water, did a few flips, before diving back in— sometimes awkwardly splashing on the surface. But I had no time for the slight pain and embarrassment.

I'd never had so much fun.

We eventually took a breather while the adults launched a game for the children. Sadly, I could only partially see from the surface. It didn't take me long to realize that this was in fact fishing training weaved into a game. They released hundreds of small spheres in the water that immediately scattered, some individually, others in groups of varying sizes. All of them moved at the same speed and according to the same patterns as a school of fish avoiding a predator. Swimming in pairs, each child holding one end of a narrow, rectangular net, they would try to capture as many of the spheres as possible, which would simply stick to the net.

After all this exertion, bellies clamoring for food finally drove us back to the village. Walking hand in hand with my husband while the raucous children ran past us, I realized what a paradise I had landed in. These people, their way of life, the future they were building for themselves was worth fighting for. And I would fight alongside them, with everything in me.

CHAPTER 12
OLIX

The next couple of days proved challenging to keep away from my Susan. Now that we had truly begun communicating and bonding, I wanted to learn more about her, her people, and of course explore our intimacy. But too much work remained to be done, and time wasn't on my side.

In a few days, a quarter of the clan would leave with me on a great hunt. We had many arrows, traps, and darts to prepare. At the same time, we had nets to mend and fishing cages to prepare for the other quarter of our clan that would set sail for fish and shellfish. For the few of the Hunters and Fishers who also crafted for the market, that didn't leave them much time to make a few additional goods before our departure. Based on the hunting plan I had laid out, our chances of returning early enough to craft some more before the public market were slim to none.

Still, I stole what time I could to spend it with my mate. Susan hadn't minded me working in a corner of her shed while making darts and coating them in a soporific agent. Luped had been around, building beautiful and strong shelves for my female that were now all filled with racks of dirt trays she called seedlings. Another set of shelves filled with a different type of dirt that she sprayed daily with water was supposed to eventually grow meat-like mushrooms.

That day, my sister installed strong hooks on beams lining the ceiling. To my shock, my Susan mixed to wet wood chips some weird thing called mycelium that resembled dried mold, then filled long plastic bags with them, tying both ends before asking me to hang them to the hook for her as they were heavy. They were actually quite light for me, but it pleased me to show my strength. The following day, she poked a bunch of holes in the bags. Nothing leaked. When I questioned her about it, she said loads of oyster mushrooms would come out of those holes. It sounded as crazy to me as her meat mushrooms. But what did I know about farming?

It shamed me to admit that Susan spending the majority of her time inside that shed, doing her seedlings and those mushroom bags was a relief. The people had begun to relax that her farming wasn't being rubbed in our faces... yet. The play days and the evenings in the Great Hall, mingling with everyone was allowing them to get to know her better.

However, the inevitable happened.

On the sixth day, Susan spent quite a bit of time assembling a strange contraption... outside. As soon as she finished, she placed it near the start of the plot of land she'd requested to farm. Her moving onto assembling another machine, this one a bit bigger, only gave me a small reprieve. I replayed in my mind all the arguments she had convinced me with and that had mollified my clan into accepting what she would do. But my stomach increasingly knotted as time ticked by. Susan was my mate, our Clan Mistress. And in a few minutes, she would start digging through dirt, like an animal... like a slave.

Maybe Mother had been right in suggesting zero tolerance. Maybe it wasn't too late to tell my female I had changed my mind. Could she not keep her farming to what she was doing here, indoors? Luped would be happy to build her more sheds so that she could grow as many things as she wanted without rolling in dirt.

With these thoughts increasingly taking root, I was reflecting on ways of broaching the subject with Susan when Zoltar's voice startled me. By the look on his face, I knew bad news had come. No words were needed for me to know I had to follow him. I gestured for him to wait a minute and warned my mate I would be leaving her side.

"Okay," she said, frowning slightly while observing me.

I packed the darts I'd been working on and, with Zoltar's help, carried them and my tools back towards the plaza. My heart sank at the sight of Surtas, the Inosh Mountains Clan Leader.

"Surtas," I said in greeting, "you are here early."

"The others will join us in two days for departure," he said.

He gestured with his chin at the field behind the Great Hall. That only made me even more nervous. Surtas wanting us away from prying ears hinted at how somber the situation was. To make matters worse, the location he chose for us to have that discussion gave us a perfect line of sight on Susan preparing to work the fields.

"The Conglomerate made me another offer," Surtas said, going straight to the point. His coppery scales looked ashen with stress, having lost their shine of old when his people thrived and prospered. "It is still meager, but higher than their previous one."

"You cannot accept!" I exclaimed.

"I may have no choice!" he hissed, his tail stiffening, while a sliver of red tinged his scales. "The next hunt and public market sales *must* be successful, or I will have no choice but to sell at least part of our lands."

"Surtas—"

"I will only offer part of the plains," he interrupted, shifting uncomfortably on his feet. "The Inosh Mountains trail and the surrounding forest will remain ours for hunting."

"They will never consent to that," Zoltar said, with barely veiled anger. "They will demand all or nothing."

"All is *not* on the table," Surtas retorted. "It will be that portion of land and nothing else."

"And what if they withdraw their offer unless you sell everything?" I asked in a soft voice.

Surtas stared at me for a moment, anger, betrayal, and despair all warring for dominance on his features. Instead of the angry outburst I had expected, his shoulders dropped, and the strong male, fearsome Hunter, and charismatic leader I'd known my whole life took on an utterly defeated expression.

"What would you have me do, Olix? My people will starve," he said in a haunted voice. "All the herds have gone. There have been no sightings whatsoever, not even small game like hoppers. *Nothing!* Worse still, even Gatherers are coming home almost empty-handed. Something is happening that's driving away the fauna and devouring the roots, leaves, and berries that used to supplement our meals."

"It has to be the Conglomerate's doing to force our hand," Zoltar said through his teeth.

"I believe it, too," I conceded, "but we have found no proof of foul play. Their people have not been seen anywhere near our forests in two years, and yet things have steadily worsened."

"It must be their technology," Zoltar argued.

"Of that, too, we have found no proof," I said, discouraged. "You know how Luped is crazy for technology. She has used all the tracking and scanning programs we could afford and found nothing. If they are indeed doing something, it is beyond our comprehension. But if we sell, they win."

"We never should have allowed off-worlders back onto our planet," Surtas said bitterly. "Life was much simpler before them. Their technology is too strong, and we are too poor to upgrade what we have or to acquire what could make us competitive. If it comes to that, and I sell my lands, my people could merge with another clan. The new wealth from the sale could spare them from having to sell as well."

That comment hurt my heart, but it was a partial solution.

"They say she grows food," Surtas suddenly said.

Startled, I followed his gaze and saw him staring at my mate in the distance. The devices Susan had been assembling now seemed fully functional. My stomach dropped as she set the first one in an upright position, hovering a few centimeters above-ground. It vaguely reminded me of a giant funnel but with a bladed hook at the bottom.

"It is a disgrace that our Clan Mistress, our Spear's mate, plays in the dirt," Zoltar hissed.

"Careful," I warned, taking a menacing step towards him. "Disrespect my Susan, and you will face my wrath."

He clenched his teeth but had the good sense of backing down. He turned his resentful gaze towards my female, then curiosity appeared to take over his displeasure. I looked back and found myself also staring in fascination. Still wearing her knee-length dress and simple closed shoes, Susan tapped a few instructions on the interface of the device. The hook underneath it straightened while retracting within itself. Seconds later, it stabbed into ground before curving again. The contraption began moving forward in a straight line, tilling the land. My female didn't follow it, turning instead towards the second device.

We watched for a short while longer. The tilling device stopped occasionally, some sort of mechanical arm extracting what resembled a sizable rock and placing it in the container on top of it, before resuming tilling. When it reached a certain distance, the claw retracted and the device moved a short distance to the side and stabbed the ground again, tilling a second row parallel to the first one.

"The Clan Mistress doesn't seem to be doing much dirt digging," Surtas said tauntingly to Zoltar. "Looks like a machine does the work."

A very good point that made my heart soar. I had dreaded seeing my Susan toiling with a pickaxe and shovel in the field.

"We are Hunters," Zoltar snapped back. "We do not work the soil."

"If it could prevent your mate, offspring, and community from starving to death, would you dig dirt, or let them perish?" Surtas challenged him.

"There are always other ways," Zoltar replied, stubbornly.

"I have yet to see those other ways you speak of," Surtas said with disdain. "You are young and impetuous, Zoltar. When it comes to the survival of your people, pride is a fool's luxury. Molzeg said Olix's off-worlder mate would save our people. Maybe she's showing us the way, but we are too stubborn to follow it. Until then, pray the Spirits that the great hunt is successful."

With these words, Surtas turned around and headed back towards the plaza, leaving me shaken. Zoltar, ever the dark cloud, hovered around, his gaze weighing on me.

"Whatever you may think of my impulsiveness, heed me well, cousin," Zoltar said. "You know how I feel about this farming business, but this isn't about me. Our people will *not work* the land. You *know* it. You have heard them speak just like I have. Your heart is in the right place, but *do not* let your female take you down this dangerous path. If you do, the people *will* remove you as our leader, and it will be all your doing."

He didn't wait for my response, and also left. My chest ached, and the same feeling of helplessness washed over me. Whatever my personal feelings, Zoltar was right. Our people would choose to sell our lands before digging dirt.

But my Susan wasn't digging dirt: her machine was.

CHAPTER 13
SUSAN

The next couple of days flew by too fast. I would have put my work on hold to spend more time with my husband before his departure, but his own work and the arrival of first Surtas, then of Clan Leader Oljek, quickly sucked up all of Olix's time. Even the last play day was cancelled. Therefore, I not only fully plowed and tilled the entire plot, I also planted my corn, wheat, bean, beet, and carrot seeds.

The whole time, an adorable little girl named Nosha lurked around. Despite her very young age, her eyes shone with intelligence and an insatiable curiosity. I could see her desire to come talk to me and ask me questions. I would have loved nothing more than to indulge her, but I pretended not to see her. I was already walking on a fine line, I couldn't risk offending her parents or the clan with perceived attempts at indoctrinating their offspring.

For the same reason, although Luped had hinted at being able to build me a sprinkler system, I decided to stick to my watering tank. The tank could take 100 gallons and could be programmed to sprinkle the specific amount of water required according to the moisture in the ground and the type of vegetable growing there.

With the sink inside the shed and the water faucet outside, I had plenty of sources of water to quickly refill it.

Granted, a proper sprinkler system would have made my life a whole lot easier, but tensions and resentment had grown noticeably since I'd begun working outdoors. The terrible situation with the Inosh Mountains Clan only made things even more tense. Thankfully, the people didn't have to see me traipsing around the field. The tiller and the water tank did all the work. I only had to refill them with seed and water as needed, which could all be done discreetly in the shadow of the shed.

Still, gathering by the Great Hall to see my husband and more than half of our clan—in an equal proportion of males and females—leave on hunting and fishing expeditions turned me into a real mess. Even Luped left. Only the Crafters, some of the Gatherers, the children, and the elders remained. It was a testament to the peaceful nature of their world that no warriors were needed to protect the village in the absence of the Hunters.

Things hadn't fully smoothed out with Yamir, but she wasn't giving me the cold shoulder anymore. The fact that I wasn't sweating my ass off in the field had earned me quite a few points towards getting back into her good graces. It was all about appearances—a lesson I had properly learned.

By the end of the first week following Olix's departure, my mother-in-law even expressed a polite interest in visiting the sheds, although I suspected it was more to spy on the extent of my heresy than anything else. Nevertheless, the sight of my mushrooms fruiting on the plastic bags impressed her, not to mention the first sprouts of my seedlings poking their heads out.

With all of this initial work done, I now had very little to do except for checking daily that my seedlings and mushroom beds had sufficient moisture and the right room temperature to thrive. As that was done in a blink, and since I didn't have to water the outdoor crops daily, that meant lots of free time on my hands. I decided to spend it with the Crafters, learning the basics of their trade as well as familiarizing myself with their products and the unique properties that made them so special.

Ever since hearing about the monthly public market, I'd been doing my homework finding out more about the species inhabiting Xecania, and especially the rich refugees that now dominated the planet's economy. One of Kayog's gifts, hidden in my belongings, had prompted this special interest. I hadn't found the reezia seeds until after the first play day and had been forced to do some research on the knowledge network to find out what they were.

When I realized they produced some sort of berries highly sought after by the Bosengi, I thought Kayog had mixed things up and gifted them to the wrong person. But then I realized how fickle and temperamental they were to grow unless handled by a highly skilled farmer. That's when I got it.

Part of me was starting to feel used in a game of chess that was far bigger than me. But the other part realized that maybe the Temern was giving me tools and options instead for me to leverage as I saw fit... or not at all. The fact that reezia berries grew very quickly, only 20 to 30 days from first planting, I could have a decent crop for the public market. I'd be cutting it short, but it was feasible. This set a plan in motion in my head that could work even better than my original one.

However, there would be no avoiding some traipsing in dirt as my seedlings began sprouting. Unwilling to antagonize Yamir and the others, especially in the absence of Luped and Olix, I opted for caution and repotted the sprouts ready for transplant into the peat pots I'd had the foresight to bring.

It required a bit of logistics to reorganize everything in a way to give the right access to light to the plants that needed it so they could thrive. But in the end, it worked out. In another couple of weeks, when they were ready to go outside, I'd be able to plant them directly into the ground with the peat pots as they were biodegradable.

By the end of the second week after Olix's departure, I was truly missing him, but also the life and energy that had reigned in the village with everyone present. Even with all the children around, running and playing—when they weren't studying or doing chores—Monkoo's spirit had become subdued, as if the world had paused while awaiting the return of its missing tribe members. Even play days had been very quiet, a majority of people doing personal stuff instead.

To my even greater distress, Yamir informed us that she had received a message from Olix informing her that they would stay away at least another week. By the sound of it, they might even return just in time for the market. That meant possibly up to nine more days before I saw my husband again.

The only mild consolation I drew out of his delayed return was the fact that my period had begun that same morning. Not only welcoming him with a 'can't touch this for the next five days' would have sucked, but I also wouldn't have been in the mood to explain to him why human females bled for five days every month without dying, and that yes, it was totally normal. While I had brought a year's supplies of liners and tampons, I would eventually have to look into how to resupply moving forward as one of the extremely rare human females on this planet.

Three days before the public market—and Olix's presumed return—I began planting my peat pot seedlings in the field outside. My tiller did most of the work, its stinger punching a hole of the appropriate size in the ground so that I only had to grab a peat pot on the hover platform following me and place it in. The tiller's mechanical arm then covered the pot with dirt before moving on to the next spot.

Despite how little effort it involved on my part, I still ended up spending a couple of hours walking in the field, which drew far too many eyes on me, especially from little Nosha. To my surprise, they weren't as hostile as I had expected—mostly curious and reserved. Once again, I wanted to believe that seeing me doing this without breaking a sweat might be gradually changing their mind about modern farming.

Had I been richer, I wouldn't even have had to place those peat pots in the ground. I would have acquired a fancier tiller-planter model that could not only plow or till three rows at the time, remove rocks and weeds, and seed, it could also transplant peat pot seedlings into the ground on its own. If my plans worked out even half as well as I hoped at the upcoming market, I would definitely buy myself an upgrade.

The next morning, Luped and the Fishers returned. No words could express the depth of the happiness I felt at seeing her pretty face and lovely blue scales. How odd that barely a month ago, when I first arrived here, I'd thought the Andturians' appearance rather freaky, and thought they all looked alike. Sure, they shared genetic features, like humans did, but their faces and bodies were distinct. My Olix and his sister were both on the gorgeous side of the Andturian aesthetic, a beauty inherited from their mother Yamir.

The Fishers' haul turned out to be pretty good. Although not record-breaking, it had everyone's spirits up. Not having much to do myself, I happily joined the efforts of fileting and salting the fish and cleaning the shellfish. Everything was then stashed in crate-like cooling units, stacked by category in the huge pantry next to the larder.

The day after tomorrow, I would rise with the sun to harvest my reezia berries and pack similar cooling units with full racks of them. Thinking about it made me a nervous wreck. I had so many hopes pinned on the success of this sale.

Despite all the work we had to do, this day and the next one dragged on forever. It also didn't help that Olix and the others still had not returned. His last communication with Yamir claimed they would make it back for the market, but they would likely cut it extremely close.

On the eve of our departure, I went back to my sheds to start preparing the cooling units and racks that I would fill with my harvest in the morning. As we would be leaving fairly early, every minute would count. Sure, I could have done it all tonight, and they would still have been fresh enough tomorrow. But the fact that they'd been picked that very morning would play a big part of my sales pitch.

As was her wont, Luped dropped by to see if I needed a hand. I'd barely known her a week before she went on that fishing expedition for three weeks. And yet, I felt closer to the Andturian female than I had ever been with any of my blood sisters. Then again, I had been purposefully raised apart to avoid painful bonds since I would be discarded in the end. Still, my heart warmed watching her take a tour of my lair.

"What you have done here is amazing," Luped whispered, awed as she stared at the shelves she'd built for me overflowing with ripe purple reezia berries. "Not even four full weeks and you have already produced all of this…"

Although she was complimenting me, Luped appeared to be musing out loud to herself. I didn't comment, pride swelling in my chest as she continued to prowl around the nursery where a number of additional vegetables would soon need to be transplanted outside. On her way in, the sight of spinach, baby carrots, green onions, and lettuce in the field, ready to be harvested had already blown her away. But coming in to see that, on top of the berries, I also had radish and oyster mushrooms ready for consumption had left her speechless.

In two to three more weeks, I'd have cucumbers, beets, zucchini, tomatoes, and squash. And then another three to four weeks after that, we'd be talking serious business with corn, wheat, and potatoes. God, how I missed potatoes!

Luped staring strangely at me pulled me out of my wandering thoughts.

"There is magic in what you do," my sister-in-law said

pensively. "Good magic. You have accomplished so much that I didn't think possible, like growing food out of wet woodchips. You have done the work of twenty with just two strange machines, and without ever straining yourself. You are proof that technology and knowledge can take our people into a better future. I do not know what you intend to do with all of this, but remember that if you need my assistance, you have it."

"Actually, there is something I wanted to run by you," I said sheepishly, grateful for this unexpected opening. She tilted her head, the vertical slit of her lizard eyes widening with curiosity. "The Crafters have told me that sales have really dropped over the past year, and especially in the last few months."

Luped nodded. "That is correct."

"I have an idea that might help their sales tomorrow, but it is all contingent on how my own sales go," I said carefully. "I am pretty certain the Bosengi will fight over these berries. If that is the case, I will try to drive them to buy some of the crafted items. But I'm totally going to wing it if and when an opportunity presents itself."

"Wing it?" Luped asked, confused.

I chuckled. "It means improvise. I'm not even quite sure how that expression came to be," I confessed. "I just need you to convince the others to play along, even if they think what I'm saying is outrageous. If things work out, everyone will get their full compensation for their goods. I promise."

"You are sounding mysterious, Susan," Luped said while lining up a couple more cooling units near the reezia berry racks. "I will tell them, but our people always show a united front in public. So, they would play along regardless, no matter how disturbed they might feel had you done it without warning them. However, see that you hold your end of the deal. Once you lose the trust of an Andturian, your chances of regaining it are slim to none. As our Clan Mistress, you have an even greater duty to uphold."

"My word is my bond," I said proudly. "And if all goes well, there will be much to rejoice about tomorrow."

"I hope you are right," Luped said. "And I hope your plans come to fruition."

She was referring to more than just successful sales. I had many plans, and God willing, they would indeed come to fruition.

We wrapped up for the night, gathering for evening meal in the Great Hall. Tomorrow, I wanted to contribute to the communal meal with spinach-lettuce-nuts-and-fruits salad, as well as sauteed oyster mushrooms with green onions. The rich soil and perfect weather here made things grow faster than expected. I would never be able to eat all of my crops by myself —not that this had ever been the plan.

Although individual dwellings didn't possess a full kitchen, we could make simple individual meals at home using a fire stone or the hot plate found in every house. But the Andturians' custom of cooking as a group for everyone would facilitate things for me to make them taste the benefits of my work. It was an interesting approach. Meal choices were decided on as a group, although a different person every day had the right to veto said choice—a power rarely used.

That night, my bed felt emptier than ever. Olix had not returned, and my hope of him showing up in the morning had seriously dwindled. I took solace in the fact that there wouldn't be another great hunt for at least a month. That meant more bonding time for the two of us. And if my plan worked, that could possibly mean a major leap in the right direction to a better future for the tribe. My biggest sorrow about the Andturians not wearing clothes was that Olix didn't even have a shirt lying around that I could cuddle with just to have his scent around me.

Despite that, sleep came quickly to me, and morning found me in high spirits. Upon exiting my house, I found the Gatherers already up, busy preparing an early breakfast. A few of the crafters were lining up mrakas to carry a lot of the merchandise. At my request, Luped had secured a shuttle for me. The pilot would come in a couple of hours to transport all of my cooling units as they were too large to comfortably sit or hang on a mraka, not to mention the fact that they would poorly travel on the road, carried by giant alien rhino-boars.

It was an expensive service to retain and constituted a major hit to my meager savings. But I had faith my sales would make up for it and then some. Initially, Yamir had frowned upon hearing I wouldn't travel the traditional way with the clan, but seeing the number of crates I was bringing, she agreed with my course of action. That I offered to carry all of their more voluminous and heavy items aboard the shuttle, as well as a few elders for whom the long journey riding a mraka was becoming challenging, further pacified her. Some elders had not participated in a public market in a few months for that specific reason.

While I didn't doubt that the clan usually rode those beasts out of tradition and enjoyment, I also believed that they often wished they could use shuttles in specific situations that warranted it, like today. They… *We* simply couldn't afford them.

For the time being…

With time ticking, I frantically picked the reezias and placed them in one-pound berry baskets, which I placed in trays of twelve inside the cooling units. Each unit took five trays secured within by hooks I could clip them onto. Although I had known my harvest would be plentiful, I never expected there would be this much in such a short time, with many small berries still growing. I'd be harvesting again in a few days, and this on a regular basis.

I'd just finished loading the seventh and last cooling unit onto the hovering platform when a commotion in the general direction of the plaza set all my senses on high alert. Setting the platform to follow, I hurried to the plaza—half-walking, half-jogging—my heart pounding in anticipation of what surprise I suspected awaited me.

Even through the crowd gathering around the returned Hunters, my eyes immediately locked onto the tall and muscular silhouette of my husband. The powerful emotion that squeezed my heart made no sense, but I didn't bother trying to analyze it. My man was home, and I was happy.

I shouted his name, involuntarily drawing quite a bit of attention to myself, and broke into a run. My body had developed a mind of its own, and my brain was just onboard for the ride. Olix stared at me with a mix of happiness, shock, and then worry as I raced towards him. I threw myself into his arms, and he caught me. His powerful arms holding me firmly, and my arms wrapped around his neck, I crushed his lips with a passionate kiss. Although our tongues didn't join the fray, Olix returned my kiss, brief though it was.

"I missed you!" I whispered before burying my face in his neck.

"I missed you, too," he replied with that deep, rumbling, and slightly sibilant voice of his.

After squeezing me one last time, Olix put me back on my feet. His darker scales made me realize he was a little embarrassed. Judging by the number of pairs of eyes ogling us like we'd both grown a second head had my own cheeks turning red. The Andturians weren't big on public displays of affection. They'd also probably never seen anyone kissing. Right now, they were likely all speculating about all the other weird things Olix and I might be doing in private.

If they only knew.

"You made it back on time," I said, trying to steer the conversation away from me making a spectacle of myself.

"Like he said he would," Yamir said proudly.

I smiled and nodded, although I silenced the annoyance I'd felt every time my mother-in-law had informed us of the status of the great hunt. Before my arrival, Olix had always relayed information to his mother when he was away so that she could pass it on to the clan. But now, it felt like he should be contacting me, his wife, instead. I shouldn't find out when my husband would come home from his mother. But that was a discussion for another time.

"We did, my mate," Olix said with a smile, although the sad glimmer in his golden eyes told me what I'd feared all along. "We must make haste putting away what we have brought back." He turned to look at his mother. "You should all leave ahead as planned with the few Hunters that are also Crafters. The rest of us will catch up."

For a brief instant, I wondered if I had misinterpreted his expression. Maybe their hunt had been successful after all, and they had a lot of game to put away. But judging by the large number of cooling units being brought back directly to the common storage room, my first presumption had been right. My heart broke for Olix.

I wanted to ask him how things had gone, how he was feeling, and if there was anything I could do... essentially be a supportive wife. However, with so many of his people around, I feared it would be like poking at a still bleeding wound. He caressed my cheek and started turning away when he noticed the hovering platform packed with crates. He gave me a questioning look. For some silly reason, I immediately felt uncomfortable, as if I'd done something illicit.

"They contain things I grew specifically to sell," I said sheepishly.

Olix didn't say anything. An unreadable expression fleeted over his reptilian features as his gaze settled on the cooling units for a few seconds before turning back towards me. He gave me a single nod. My stomach twisted. I didn't know how to interpret what had just happened. Did he feel betrayed? Did he feel like I was rubbing the failure of his hunt in his face? Did...?

The sound of the approaching shuttle coming to taxi my stuff and me to the market forced my attention away from my husband. This was not the reunion I had hoped for. Our relationship was still too fragile to have already undergone that long separation and for him to return with this much stress.

Now, I didn't even know how to feel about the market anymore. What if a resounding success only rubbed more salt in the wound?

Distraught, I supervised the loading of my harvest. The shuttle proved even more spacious than I had anticipated, allowing us to pack it with all of the larger items the clan hoped to sell, from big, ornate wooden bowls and plates, to sculpted vases and statues, to low, cushioned benches similar to the ones commonly used by the Andturians, although scaled slightly smaller. On top of all that, there was enough room left for Yamir, me, and five elder Andturians, including Molzeg. I wished Luped and Olix could have traveled with us, but it made more sense for them to ride the mrakas. Since they wouldn't be burdened with a passenger like me, they'd be able to travel a lot faster.

The riders left shortly before our shuttle took flight. We completed the journey mostly in silence. Yamir kept a neutral expression, but I could feel her pain and worry for her son and clan as a whole. Despite our differences, I liked the older female. She was a devoted mother to her children and her people in general. I'd never been close to my own mother. In this instant, I wanted to pull my mother-in-law into my arms and tell her that all would be well—we would get through this together. But now wasn't the time, not with the others packed with us in the shuttle and within hearing range.

Still, it took barely fifteen minutes instead of the more than one hour ride on a mraka. This perfectly suited my purpose as we not only got to settle our kiosk early, but it would give me time to do some reconnaissance.

"With your permission, Yamir, I would like to set my stall in the middle, with the furniture and houseware at my left and the weapons and jewelry at my right," I said carefully.

She slightly recoiled, her eyes narrowing while she pondered. "Luped says you have a plan to help sales today," Yamir said without answering my request.

I nodded. "If my berries are well-received, I believe it will enable me to help the Crafters sell more."

"I struggle with understanding your ways, Susan of Meterion," Yamir said in a slightly tired voice. "It troubles me that you are what you are, but your skills cannot be denied. I believe you have genuine affection for my son and our people. Both are hurting right now. If you think this position could help bring a better outcome to this day, you have my support."

"Thank you," I said with gratitude. "I cannot promise what will happen today, but I will try my best."

Yamir's expression softened. "Only Seers can predict the future, and even then, it is often cryptic. Your best is all that anyone can ask for. The rest lies in the hands of the Spirits."

On these final words, she went on to help the elders set up their tables and display their goods on each side of my own humble table—all of which were provided by the venue. Where my companions piled up their goods on the tables, on the floor in front and around them, and had tall standing panels at the back onto which they would hang jewelry once the others arrived, I had a single table. I covered it with a light beige tablecloth and placed my cooling units under it to keep my place clean and uncluttered, but also to hide just how much stock I had left.

As patrons wouldn't show up for another hour at least, I seized this opportunity of our early arrival to investigate the other stalls being set up at the market as well as take a peek at a few of the tourist shops inside the spaceport. To the extent possible, I'd been doing my homework online, finding out what products the Conglomerate was selling here and at what price points.

But nothing beat seeing it firsthand. What I saw further rein-forced my determination to carry out my plan. I acquired some overpriced blank tokens at one of the stores which could have a value imprinted on them with a basic com or datapad.

When I returned to my table, I sweet talked Kuani—one of the housewage Crafters—to lend me one of her medium-sized presentation plates made of aldomyan wood. The dark grey wood, with tiny streaks of dark red, was stunning. Smoothly polished and embellished with finely chiseled motifs and lumi-nous stones, it was a beauty to behold. A very thin layer of the same sotomac resin Olix had used to seal my blood into his wristbands and weapon had been applied to the plate so that it would never lose its shine. I made it the centerpiece of my table. I also snagged two small bowls from her in the same style as the plate, and a stunning fork—that seemed taken straight out of a fondue set—with a handle made of sculpted mraka tusk.

I was getting beyond antsy to take out my berries, but it was still too early. As the first of our clanmates started arriving on their mrakas, I busied myself encoding my tokens and placing them inside the two bowls.

Olix arrived at the same time the organizers of the event announced the customers would be allowed in shortly. My heart skipped a beat, excitement, and trepidation warring within me. Forcing myself to focus, I opened one of my cooling units, and took out two pounds of berries that I carefully washed at one of the eight water stations provided for the merchants of the market. I also filled a bottle with water so that I could spray a fine mist on my fruits throughout the day to keep them looking fresh and mouth-watering.

When I began placing them in the center platter, Olix came near my stall, a slight frown marring his face at the sight of my mostly empty station. He appeared to want to ask me what was wrong, but someone calling his name prevented him from doing

I MARRIED A LIZARDMAN

so. I hated that we hadn't had a chance to discuss my plan. I only hoped things would go well, and that he would be proud of me.

After displaying my sample tasting berries, I removed the entire contents of my first cooling unit, placing two full trays on each side of the centerpiece, and lining individual one-pound baskets in front of it. Addressing a silent prayer to all the powers that be, I began the waiting game.

CHAPTER 14
OLIX

I wanted this day to be over. Although the great hunt had not been a complete disaster, it hadn't been even remotely as successful as we had needed it to be. I wished to be in my sleeping nest, losing myself in my mate, and forgetting for a short while all the troubles weighing on my shoulders. But now, even Susan had gone to the market to sell goods. I didn't know how to handle that.

A part of me felt betrayed. Our agreement had been for her to grow produce dear to her people that was otherwise impossible for her to acquire here. There had never been discussions of her producing food to be sold. At the same time, it was fair for her to seek a means of earning some credits in order to purchase things for herself that couldn't be found here. After all, she had mentioned wanting to upgrade one of her pieces of farming equipment.

I took a stroll through her field, my jaw dropping at the sight of all the fat, leafy greens covering rows of the land I'd allocated to her. The presence of Surtas shadowing me only twisted the knife in the raw wound of my failure. Setting foot inside her sheds robbed me of voice. The amount of food Susan had managed to produce by herself in such a short time left me reeling. None of it was familiar to my people, but it looked fresh, healthy, and quite appealing.

I should be providing for my mate, but she had no need of me.

"She had seven cooling units full of food, and there's still all of this left?" Surtas said with an odd mix of anger and bitterness.

My head jerked towards him, and I eyed the Inosh Mountain Clan Leader warily.

"In one month, she produced so much food she can sell some of it. We canvassed the forest for three weeks and barely brought back anything," Surtas said. "What does that tell you?"

"We don't even know that it will sell," I argued.

"That's not the point, and you know it!" Surtas snapped angrily.

No, that wasn't the point. "It is not me you need to convince, Surtas," I said in a tired voice. "Maybe her food will sell well at the market. Then all the clans will get to see it."

"And then?" he insisted.

"And then we will advise," I replied in a calm voice. "But tell me, my friend, would your own clan agree to work our lands to grow food as my mate has?"

His shoulders slumped. "Right now, no," he reluctantly admitted. "I pray the Spirits your mate has a resounding success at the market, and that it will open the people's eyes. I mean, look at all of this food!" he added, waving at the shelves filled with berries, maturing seedlings, and the wide troughs filled with dirt where large, flat mushrooms were growing. "She will never be able to eat all of it on her own."

"She isn't going to," I said. I'd begun to suspect her not so hidden agenda right from the beginning and received confirmation from one of the Gatherers while putting away what little meat we'd brought back. "Tonight, she will prepare some of her human food for everyone at evening meal so that we can sample it."

"Clever female," Surtas said, a hopeful smile stretching his lips.

"Clever, yes. But I fear she will face great disappointment," I said with a frown. "The people will appreciate the gesture, but I doubt it will yield the result she is hoping for. In truth, I'm surprised she didn't bring a variety of this produce to the market for sale as well. After all, there is a small number of human residents that work at some of the resorts and at the spaceport. Surely, they would have been interested in such goods."

"I am glad she did not. I believe the Spirits sent your mate to us. Today is important. I feel it in my bones," Surtas said with a conviction that sparked an irrational hope within me.

"May you be right," I said.

Casting one final look at the bounty growing inside the shed, I headed back to the plaza to mount my mraka and head to the market, Surtas in my wake. Much could happen if my Susan's venture proved successful. In light of our hunt's partial failure, would it embolden her into trying to convert our people to her ways?

Would that be a bad thing?

Had she come to us in a generation or two from now, it would have been a great thing. While I was personally softening to the potential of what her skill could do for our people, the majority of our clan would not bend, no matter the cost. A plethora of scenarios on how the day would end depending on the outcome of the market played in a loop in my head as we raced to the spaceport.

By the time we reached it, my heart tightened viewing the crowd already amassed outside the venue. As with every month of late, the same type of customers were gathering, all of them talking about the off-worlder goods they were looking to acquire. Over the past couple of years, the number of native stalls had steadily decreased to be replaced by foreigners trying to flood our market with their products. I held no hopes of a good outcome today—a second blow I could have truly done without.

I made my way to the market where every merchant was finalizing their set up for the imminent opening. Finding Susan's table almost empty distressed me. As much as I feared her success, I also didn't want her to fail, not only to spare her the disappointment, but also because it would likely undermine her already shaky standing among the people. Word had quickly spread that she would be attempting to help our sales. Although no one could fault her if that failed, an unhealthy level of anticipation had been building among my clanmates.

However, the first couple of customers roaming nearby drew my attention. I didn't want to hope, having been let down so many times before, and yet I couldn't help it. As always, they strolled nearby, close enough to get an idea of what was on offer, but not so much that it would allow us to strike a conversation with them.

And then, the first couple of Bosengis dropped by.

Their lukewarm interest in the weapons and jewelry on display completely transformed the minute the female took a whiff of the berries. Her beady eyes widened, the small holes on her flat face that served as nostrils flared, and the external gills around the upper side of her round face stood on ends, making her head look like a strange star.

"Reezia!" she whispered, half-running to Susan's table.

Her partner appeared stunned and quickly followed her. We could literally see their heartbeats accelerating through their semi-translucent skins as they stared at the bounty laid before my mate.

"Can I interest you in some reezia berries harvested fresh from this morning?" Susan asked in a gentle voice.

"From this morning?" the female exclaimed in disbelief.

"Yes, Madam," Susan said proudly. "Grown right here on Xecania, in the Monkoo Valley. Care to taste one?"

"Most certainly, yes," the female said, licking her lips in anticipation.

Susan carefully stabbed a plump berry in the presentation plate with one of the forks crafted by Kuani and extended it towards the Bosengi female. She plucked it off the fork with two fingers and shoved the berry into her mouth. She no sooner began to chew than she closed her eyes, her body shaken by a powerful shiver. A disturbingly sensual moan rose from her throat and a tremor coursed through her external gills. Her pale, yellow skin turned a brighter shade of yellow.

Her companion licked his lips and stared at my mate with a greedy and hopeful expression. But Susan was already stabbing another berry for him this time. The male's reaction reflected that of his female. The latter, having already swallowed the fruit she'd been given, was eyeing the bounty on the table with an almost feral greed.

"I would like to buy some of your berries," she said to Susan while elbowing her mate.

"Yes," he said, also looking like he could barely refrain from gorging on everything in front of him. "I will give you 30 marks for a basket."

30 marks?!

It took all of my willpower to keep a neutral expression on my face. That was an outrageous price for this little basket of fruits. Some of our Crafters' ornate leather bracelets, that took days of hard work, sold for only 20 marks. And even then, we struggled to find buyers.

To my shock, Susan recoiled, all friendly demeanor fading from her face as she cast an offended look at the male.

"I'm sorry. I thought you were here to do serious business," Susan said in a slightly clipped tone.

This time, I had to bite my tongue not to ask my mate what

was wrong with her. By the looks our clanmates were casting her way, they were also wondering what madness had taken over her, while doing their best to hide their shock.

"Thirty marks is a good price!" the male exclaimed, clearly displeased to be so rebuffed.

"Thirty marks is insulting, at best," Susan replied, staring at him with an icy gaze. "You pay 45 marks without blinking for frozen, genetically engineered reezias, filled with pesticides, and grown in an industrial complex, but offer me 30 lousy marks for organically grown reezias, in accordance with Bosengi traditional methods, pesticide-free, and freshly picked this very morning? Clearly, you are no connoisseur."

While the male opened and closed his mouth repeatedly, at a loss for words to have been thus called out by my mate, Susan turned her attention to another group of Bosengis, this time a trio of two females and one male.

"Organic and fresh from this morning?" one of the new females asked my mate, having overheard the conversation.

"Yes, Madam," Susan said with a glowing smile. "Would you care to taste?"

"Absolutely!" the female responded.

Susan gave each of the three newcomers a single berry, prompting the same reaction as with the first couple.

"This is a true taste of home," the female said with disbelief. "How have you accomplished this? Reezia is extremely hard to grow without a perfect technique."

"I am an expert farmer, born and raised on Meterion," Susan said proudly.

"A daughter of Meterion! That explains it," the female said, a glimmer of admiration sparkling through her small, round eyes. "I will give you 60 marks for a basket."

"It is 70 marks for a single basket," Susan said apologetically. "However, if you buy six, you get a token for a discount of up to 30 marks on any of the Andturian crafted goods on sale here," she added, waving at the Crafter tables on each side of her own little stall. "But if you buy a full tray of twelve baskets, I will lower the price to 60 marks per basket—which means you actually get two and half baskets for free—AND I will give you a token for a discount of up to 60 marks to purchase one of our other goods."

I felt faint. Aside from the outrageous price she'd been offered, then increased for things that would be consumed in minutes, the clever ploy Susan was using to drive traffic to our Crafters robbed me of words.

"70 marks!?" the male of the first couple exclaimed, sounding offended. "That's ludicrous!"

The female of the trio cast him a sideways glance. "What is it, Wolny? Your wallet cannot afford quality?"

The couple gasped, the male outraged, and his female giving him a warning glance that he had better defend their honor. I barely repressed a snort, but one of our clanmates failed to do so. The Bosengis were a wealthy and very ostentatious species. One was expected to make a loud display of their success in every way.

Without waiting for their response, the trio leader turned back to my Susan. "So, if I take two trays, you will lower the cost per basket at 50 marks each?"

My mate chuckled and shook her head. "No, 60 marks is the lowest I can go considering the hard work involved in growing such delicacies. However, for each tray you buy, you will get an extra token for a discount of up to 60 marks for the goods of our Crafters."

She pursed her lips and cast a glance at the crafted goods. Her gaze lingered on the standing panel with some of the most expensive jewelry we had on offer.

"So, if I bought these four trays you have for sale, I would get a 240 marks discount, meaning I could buy these two necklaces at 100 marks each and a pair of bracelets at 20 marks each?" she asked.

I held my breath. That would be a wonderful sale. But that was short-lived. My heart sank when my female shook her head.

"Not exactly," Susan said. "You cannot stack the tokens that way. It is one token per purchase, hence why I said the discount is *up to* 60 marks. So, if you want one of those one-of-a-kind, premium necklaces at 100 marks, you will give one token and pay the difference of 40 marks. However, you could get one of the more affordable models at 60 marks or less, which would cost you nothing but the token. That said, if you use a token on something that costs 30 marks, you lose the balance."

It took me a moment reflecting on this system—which seemed complicated at first glance—to realize how clever it was. Had the customers been able to stack the tokens, they could have indeed acquired high end items for free, or a slew of cheaper ones.

"This feels somewhat unfair," she complained.

"How is it unfair?" Susan asked, looking at her with an air of complete innocent confusion—that I knew for a fact to be fake. "I'm *gifting* you the ability to get up to 60% discount on hand-crafted jewelry made with the noblest materials found on Xeca-nia, simply for buying some of my fruits. I doubt you will find any other merchant making you such a generous offer."

"They're not that special," the female from the first disgrun-tled couple interjected. "We've bought similar jewelry for a cheaper price."

"With all due respect, Madam," Susan said in a polite, but somewhat patronizing tone, "the only similarities between the necklace you are currently wearing and the ones my clanmates are selling, is the style. I'm afraid you've been duped into buying a cheap knock-off."

"Cheap knock-off?" she exclaimed, outraged.

It was indeed a cheap knock-off. Any Andturian could see it. But how did my Susan know this?

Susan nodded with an apologetic expression. "I'm afraid so. See how the leather has darkened? A true Andturian piece of jewelry—or any of their other crafts for that matter—does not discolor with time," my mate accurately explained. "The ribbed pearls that adorn them are actually lillian shells. You're wearing a beautiful blue sarong. I would have expected you to make the shells match its color. But you can't because those shells are synthetic reproductions. Whereas Andturian jewelry and weapons are adorned with the real thing. Yamir, will you show them?"

My mother eagerly picked up one of the most expensive necklaces on display and came to stand next to Susan. By now, a few more Bosengis, including a handful of humans, and Drantians had gathered around to observe and listen.

Using a heating wand, my mother aimed it at the female's dress for the sensor to capture the exact color. She then carefully rubbed the tip of the wand on the shells of the necklace which quickly took on the same hue. A collective gasp rose from the crowd.

"Lillians are a shellfish found in certain bodies of water here, on Xecania. They exude heat to change the color of their shells as camouflage," Mother explained to the female. "Once set, the color remains until a noticeable variation in heat triggers another change. What you are wearing are not real lillian shells."

She gave her an apologetic smile, cast a glance towards my mate, then headed back to her stand—but not before I noticed the very pleased expression she was attempting to hide.

"I will take the four trays and the tokens," the female from the trio stated, gesturing at her male companion to pay Susan.

"What? Wait? You can't take everything and leave nothing for the others," the stingy male she'd called Wolny exclaimed.

"You had your chance, but chose to cling to your credits," the female responded with a shrug. "Your loss."

"It's okay, I have some more," Susan replied reassuringly.

She quickly concluded the transaction, my head spinning at the sight of the crazy amount of credits being handed to my mate for things that only required a bit of water once every other day for three weeks. I sprang into action, pulling another cooling unit from under the table, and took out a tray for Susan. She beamed at me with gratitude and nodded her approval when I placed four of them on the table, the same way she had previously set the others.

Watching the first trio spending all four of their tokens on some of the most expensive jewelry of my Crafters had my throat constricting with emotion. While a few humans and other species bought a basket or two, the majority of the customers were Bosengi, buying full trays.

However, a number of the tourists actually stopped at our Crafter stalls to buy without tokens—on top of the Bosengis with tokens. It was eye-opening the number of customers asking questions about the trinkets they had bought at the tourist shops of the resort and spaceport, thinking them authentic, only to find out none of them had the unique properties of our true products. More sales were thus concluded.

Too soon, my mate sold out her thirty-five trays. Many of the Bosengis placed more orders with her, not only for reezia berries, but also for other products from their homeworld they couldn't easily procure here. Although she didn't commit to anything, she promised to investigate that possibility. In the meantime, with my consent, she had agreed that the Bosengis could come by the village twice a week—with an appointment—to buy that day's berry harvest.

By the time the market closed, Susan made more than 25,000 marks—2,000 of which she redistributed to the Crafters in compensation for the tokens she had handed out. I made 4,000 marks from my weapons sales, twenty-five times more than my usual proceeds on any given market day. The other Crafters also sold more than 50% of their inventory, many with special requests for the next market.

The return home was beyond festive. The Spirits had heard our prayers. My mate had saved the day.

CHAPTER 15
SUSAN

I was flying high. Everything had gone so well, far beyond my wildest dreams. Even as I flew back to the village with the elders and my mother-in-law, I couldn't wipe the stupid grin off my face. My companions kept talking in excited voices, switching back and forth between Universal and their mother tongue, so carried away they forgot I didn't understand it. But I didn't mind. They weren't trying to exclude me, but were simply overjoyed by their long overdue success.

There was something magical about seeing people happy and basking in that aura of joy. Knowing that I had a hand in making it happen made it all the more amazing. And yet, I had little merit. Their products were fantastic, but disloyal competition from the Conglomerate had undermined my new people who knew and understood so little about marketing. I fully intended to address this matter in the upcoming days and file formal complaints with the UPO.

The swift flight home allowed me to get a head start on preparing my contribution to tonight's meal. Between the market's success and the dishes I would present, I held strong hopes that this would mark a radical shift in the Andturians' way of thinking when it came to farming. With the kind of credits I had made with just this limited amount of reezia berries, we could be making a killing by diversifying the products on offer and producing them in larger quantities. The tourist resorts alone could represent a huge market for us.

Bubbling with excitement, as soon as I finished unloading and putting away my empty cooling units, I made a beeline for my shed to harvest oyster mushrooms, green onions, and some herbs, and then out to the field to pick some lettuce and spinach. I was just finishing putting them in a hover basket when Yamir's soft voice startled me. I had not seen her approach so lost I had been in my thoughts.

"I did not know what to expect today. I had hoped for even a tenth of the success that was achieved," she said looking at me with a strange expression. "Because of what you did, Clan Leader Surtas will not sell his lands tomorrow as he had originally planned. The proceeds they have received will allow them to hold for at least two more months. Two more months means two more public markets. Even if they are only half as successful as today's, it will be enough for all of us to thrive and retain our lands. You have taught us much this day. You are a great Clan Mistress and a loving partner to my son. Thank you for what you have done. I am proud to call you Daughter."

Too many emotions ran through me, leaving me voiceless. Tears pricked my eyes as she gazed at me with affection. In that instant, I badly wanted a hug. My own mother had never claimed me with such pride and affection—not a third daughter. But Andturians weren't big on the displays of affection. Yamir simply smiled then turned around and left.

I took a moment to compose myself before heading to the Great Hall where the Hunters and Gatherers, who hadn't attended the public market, had already begun preparing the evening meal. It was fascinating watching them roasting an entire warbull on the spit—the Xecania version of a deer—in the back kitchen. Working alongside the other Gatherers, I started washing and cutting my vegetables, using some of the local fruits and nuts for my spinach and lettuce salad, as well a mix of human and Andturian spices for my sauteed mushrooms.

Seeing them eye me with undisguised curiosity only pushed me to make even more of a show of my preparations as I happily discussed with them the various recipes I would make in the future once more of my vegetables had grown. They seemed particularly interested in moussaka and potatoes in general.

When I finally started cooking the mushrooms, my own mouth watered from the delicious aroma. Despite the large number of people present with the visiting clans for the market, I didn't fear running out. In fact, I had so many mushrooms, I intended to gift some to our neighboring clans before they left.

Having finished my own preparations, I was helping the Gatherers divide the other side dishes into equal portions to be placed on warming plates, when Olix walked into the back kitchen. My stomach did a somersault when he grabbed my hand and hauled me after him out of the room under the amused stares of the others.

I didn't have to ask to know what they were thinking. When the Fishers party had returned two days ago, the couples who had been separated for those few weeks had disappeared from view shortly thereafter. It didn't take a rocket scientist to figure out why. As Andturians didn't do the whole foreplay thing and both males and females self-lubricated at will, they just got straight down to business and were done in no time. That definitely didn't happen between Olix and me. With dinner about to be served, he couldn't possibly intend to…?

We only made it as far as the back of the building. Olix pushed me against the wall, lifted me up so my legs would wrap around his waist, then crushed my lips in a passionate kiss… tongue and all. Gone was the somber and distressed aura that had weighed him down since his arrival. Man, I looooved kissing my husband. It was all the stranger that his scaly lips felt nothing like a human's, but I couldn't get enough of him. Breaking the kiss, he tilted my head back to kiss and lick my neck.

Today, for the first time, he scraped his pointy teeth over my skin. The sensation resonated straight in my core. Andturians were biters. Their thick scales protected them from harm—you'd have to really give a good chomp to pierce through. But as mine was super fragile in comparison, Olix had seriously held back with me. Despite the excessive care he displayed, it thrilled me that he was taking more risks with us, calculated though they were.

Although his cock had not extruded—we couldn't, seeing how exposed we were to anyone who might walk by—Olix rubbed his pelvis against mine, while fondling my breast and kissing me again. A moan escaped me as I began to throb, aching to be filled. That sound appeared to snap Olix out of his lustful haze as he immediately stopped what he was doing. His golden eyes—darkened by desire—bore into mine.

"You awaken a burning hunger in me, my mate," Olix said, his voice sounding even deeper than usual. "I cannot wait for the meal to end so that I can take you back to our sleeping nest."

I licked my lips nervously, my inner walls contracting in anticipation.

"I cannot wait either," I said in a breathy voice.

He chuckled and purred in that strange way of his that mixed with a rattling sound. It had creeped me out the first time I'd heard it. But now, I found it sexy as fuck.

"After evening meal," he said, his voice full of promise.

He kissed me one last time before putting me down. However, instead of taking me right back inside, Olix stared at me for a moment, studying my features as if he was seeing me for the first time.

"Thank you for chasing away the dark clouds that were engulfing this day," he suddenly said, his voice deep with emotion. "Thank you for choosing me as your mate despite the hardships that awaited you. Thank you for being a better partner to me than I can ever be to you. It shames me that you give me and my people so much when I have so little to offer you in return. I—"

"You *have* already given me so much more than you realize, Olix," I said, cupping his face in my hands, my heart filling with affection for him. "You've given me things I've never had before: a forever home where I don't have to live in fear of getting kicked out when a certain date comes. A sister who supports me and genuinely wants a warm relationship with me. A mother who proudly claims me as her daughter, even though she doesn't fully understand me. A people to belong to and for whom I can make a difference. You've given me purpose, safety, and you've given me you—a kind and affectionate husband who does his best to make me happy. I don't need material things from you. What you've given me is far more precious and invaluable."

A powerful emotion crossed his features as he gazed upon me in a way that made my insides liquefy and my knees wobble. He drew me into his embrace and gave me the sweetest, bone crushing hug, his lips brushing against my right ear.

"You are the greatest blessing the Spirits could have ever bestowed upon me," Olix whispered.

After kissing my ear, he released me and led me back inside the Great Hall, holding my hand. Although the people found that type of interaction strange, they still smiled with amused expressions as we headed to the main table. To my utter relief, the Andturians didn't launch into the endless speeches I had expected. Everyone knew why we were celebrating.

As the Gatherers began bringing the plates to be shared, my heart fluttered again. Seeing large bowls of my salad and sauteed mushrooms being served alongside the other dishes on every table had me dying with nerves. It messed with me all the more when, as soon as Pawis placed them on our table, Olix went straight for a healthy serving of both, ignoring his traditional dishes. I held my breath as he took a first bite of the spinach salad. Seeing his shoulders subtly relax as he began chewing sent a wave of relief coursing through me. I realized then that my husband had been just as worried that he'd dislike my dishes.

He took a couple more bites before grinning at me. I puffed out my chest seeing a similar reaction from Yamir and Luped, as well as others around the room. But my mushrooms cinched it. Andturians ate a lot of mushrooms, although different from the oyster ones I'd grown. I had slightly modified my usual recipe to include some of their spices. When Olix took his first mouthful, the narrow slit of his lizard eyes widened so much, it almost looked like a human pupil, and that rattling moan he did, usually when I pleasured him, rose from his throat.

I burst out laughing, my face heating with happiness when he chowed down the portion he had put in his plate, his gaze going back to the shared bowl, visibly itching to get a second serving. Luped didn't shy away and took more, prompting him to do so as well. Although the Andturians enjoyed the salad and cleaned all of their shared bowls, the mushrooms were the star.

"This is beyond delicious, my mate," Olix said, looking longingly at the empty mushroom plate as if he wanted to lick it. "Seeing how you had many mushrooms growing on those hanging bags, you will be able to prepare this dish often, yes?"

I chuckled. "Yeah, those mushrooms grow fast. But if everyone wants to eat some regularly, I'll have to make a few more bags to help maintain a steady supply," I replied, beaming.

"I will bring you more woodchips in the morning, and you can tell me where to build more hooks," Luped immediately offered.

It's working! It's freaking working!

"And I will hook them up for you when they are ready," Olix offered, not wanting to be one-upped by his sibling.

"Sounds like a plan," I said with a silly grin.

To my surprise, the celebration appeared set to continue well after the meal. Unlike on my wedding day, the visiting tribes didn't leave as soon as the meal ended but chose to spend the night. A few crashed at some of our villagers' dwellings, but most of the Hunters chose to sleep under the stars on the plaza, as was their wont when out hunting.

But Olix and I bowed out as soon as the Gatherers began clearing the tables. I had probably downed a few glasses of berry cider too many. I wasn't drunk, but certainly a little tipsy, and most definitely extremely horny. My husband seemed to be in the exact same frame of mind. This time, we didn't make it to the shower. The moment Olix had taken my hand to lure me towards the house, I'd started getting wet.

The minute the door closed behind us, I made a beeline for the sturdy communal table in our family room while pulling down my panties. I kicked them off at the same time as my sandals and sat at the edge of the table.

"I need you inside of me now," I said in an urgent voice, lifting the knee-length skirt of my dress.

Desire and confusion warred on Olix's face, his nostril flaring at the scent of my arousal.

"Extrude," I urged him, pulling him to me by his chest harness still adorned with my blood.

"What about four play?" he asked, hesitantly.

I grabbed his right hand and placed it between my thighs. His palm cupped my sex, while two of his fingers partially sank inside of me, feeling the slickness he had triggered. He made a rattling hissing sound, his face taking on a dark expression filled with lust.

"You already lubricated for me," Olix said, his voice taking on a growling tone that had my nipples hardening in a blink.

My husband extruded. His thick and long shaft stood proudly —almost menacingly—his own pre-lubrication making the thin scales covering it gleam under the light bathing the room. Olix slipped his arms under my knees, lifting them up while dragging me closer to the edge. I gasped, slapping a hand on top of the table for support while the other settled under his quills to rest on his nape.

Olix pushed himself inside me quickly, not savagely, but with noticeably less patience and care than previously. Although he was still a tight fit, and despite the three-weeks separation, my body had begun adapting to him. It still burned a little going in, but I welcomed it, impatient for him to unleash his passion on me.

My man crushed my lips in a hungry kiss, his tongue dominating mine as he started moving inside of me. Those scales and that crazy hump on top of his shaft were driving me insane with pleasure. In seconds, his cock was pounding into me. All I could do was cling to him and moan into his mouth while he wrecked me.

Olix growled a few words in his language, and something shifted. Without stopping to rock in and out of me, he broke the kiss, forced me onto my back on the table, and lifted my legs over his shoulders.

"Touch yourself," he ordered, his hands settling on my hips before he began thrusting inside me at an even greater pace.

We'd only watched porn videos once together since my husband had confessed trying to learn how to please me that way. It had been an amazing bonding experience. Seeing a woman masturbate while a man fucked her had turned him on like crazy. Since then, he'd taken to asking me to rub my clit and fondle my breasts while he took me. As much as I loved pleasing him, it made me climax too quickly. By themselves, the scales and bump on his cock had me skirting the edge of ecstasy in no time. Touching myself on top was a killer. And sure enough, moments after I complied to his request, I fell apart.

Olix shouted in pleasure but didn't relent, his fingers taking up where mine had left off while I rode the waves of bliss. My man loved how my inner walls contracted around him when I climaxed. As soon as I started to come back down, he suddenly pulled out of me, lowered my legs, and then flipped me onto my stomach. I yelped as the room spun around me. Before I knew what was happening, his right foot pushed mine to the side, spreading my legs, and he penetrated me from behind in one powerful thrust.

I cried out in both pleasure and pain. He seemed to be almost possessed as he took me in a frenzy. Olix had gone full Andturian on me, his retractable claws poking out, stinging the tender flesh of my hips. Fear, pleasure, and blind lust had me pushing myself up on my arms and rocking back and forth to meet him, thrust for thrust. It was our first time doing it like this. He'd never felt so big and so deep inside of me. When he fisted my hair, yanking my head back, and his sharp teeth pressed onto the fleshy part of my shoulder, a blinding light exploded before my eyes, and I fell apart again. If not for Olix holding me, I would probably have collapsed.

He continued to pound into me until he finally found his own release. My limbs felt like jelly when he collected me in his arms and carried me to the bathroom to wash us both. That ended up taking longer than expected when he took me again against the shower wall. That night, he woke me a few more times to have his way with me. My voice was shot from having screamed so much in ecstasy, and my pussy was wrecked from having been so thoroughly fucked.

It was good to have my mate home.

CHAPTER 16

SUSAN

I woke up feeling wonderfully sore, but disappointed that Olix had already left again. Not only was my man an early bird, but I'd also discovered that Andturians only needed an average of five to six hours of sleep to be fully rested. Many were content with a measly four hours. When I came out of the house, I was shocked to realize that I had slept in well past noon. To my dismay, the visiting clans had already left before I could give them some fresh mushrooms to take home with them.

To make matters worse, the chatter on the plaza all but crushed me. It had been stupid of me to think yesterday would have finally made them see the light. Instead of incentivizing them to embrace farming, yesterday's success had galvanized them into crafting even more goods for the next market, with bigger and bolder designs, considering some of the requests of the customers. With the Bosengis being the biggest spenders, they were all talking of crafting more premium items—jewelry, weapons, and even the type of sarong and togas the bipedal, axolotl-looking species wore.

While I'd been sleeping, the Crafters had been drafting some undeniably gorgeous sketches. The Hunters were cleaning and polishing bones, horns, hooves, and claws, or tanning the hides that would be used by the Crafters. Olix was personally working on a massive pair of tusks. As most of the younger and stronger Gatherers were missing, I could only assume they'd gone to mine ore or cut timber.

The warm smiles everyone cast my way when I emerged from the house made me feel horrible for failing to share their enthusiasm. It didn't make sense to me to waste the incredible wealth of the lands they owned to craft trinkets to sell to tourists.

Andturians had no ambitions of enriching themselves. They chose to live a simple life. They only wanted comfort and the ability to meet the needs of their people. Farming was more in line with that mentality. On top of that, not only would it solve all of their food problems, it would also give them the credits needed to acquire the technology that would allow them to remain on a level with the rest of the planet.

"Sister!" Luped exclaimed, walking towards me along with Olix.

The expression on their faces immediately had all of my senses in full alert, especially when a number of the Crafters also gathered nearby. I cast an inquisitive look at my husband before turning back to my sister-in-law.

"The clan discussed while you were sleeping," Olix said. "Yesterday, you received a lot of orders from the Bosengis, and the clans really loved your mushrooms. Since you have already used most of the space in your two sheds for your mushrooms and reezia berries, we were thinking you might need a bigger shed. If so, we would be happy to build it for you."

My jaw dropped.

"We could make a more modern design," Luped said enthusiastically. "Instead of you trying to adapt to the existing building, we could create one specifically designed for your needs."

"And with the Bosengis saying they want to fly here once or twice a week to buy your fresh berries—and anything else you might add in the future—we could build you a permanent store near the landing pad," Olix said with a grin. "It could have vertical cooling units so that you could slide the trays in like shelves instead of stacking them."

"That way, on the days you want to rest, you could only fill the units with the berries you want to sell, and one of the elders could handle the store for you," Yamir added.

I felt overwhelmed. This was what I had wished FOR THEM! To grow large enough quantities and varieties of produce that they would set up a permanent market that people would fly here to buy either raw produce, or processed ones like jams, pickled vegetables, and flour, to name a few.

It broke my heart that they still considered farming an 'off-worlder' activity, but not something a true Andturian would ever 'lower' himself to do. At the same time, it deeply moved me to see how the whole clan had rallied to do something like this for me.

"I... I don't know what to say," I replied, tears pricking my eyes. "I'm incredibly touched that you would consider going to so much trouble for me. No one has ever done something like this for me. That is beyond generous. I'm speechless."

"It is no trouble at all," Luped said with a dismissive gesture. "We're all pretty excited!"

"You are a valued member of our clan," Olix said affection-ately. "Andturians always do for each other when needed. The only thing you need to say is yes, my Susan."

"We have already done some sketches of what the shop could look like, unless you have a different idea that we would be happy to build instead," Yamir said, showing me on a datapad a breathtaking concept made of wood and stone.

The detailed sketch even hinted at the bas-relief sculpting that would be done in both the wood and stone to beautify the building. Inside, a large, ornate counter divided the front and back of the store. The front had a series of low benches serving as a waiting area, whereas the back had a generous number of vertical cooling units and shelves for whatever other products I might decide to sell later.

"This is absolutely perfect," I whispered, my voice trembling from emotion.

"Then it is decided!" Olix said with a toothy grin. "You will describe to Luped your dream shed—or rather greenhouse—and we will build it, too."

And just like that, the non-Crafters among the clan ended up devoting the greater part of the next couple of weeks building my new and improved workspaces.

With the insane proceeds I had made from the first market, I bought myself my dream all-in-one tilling-seeding-weeding-and-transplanting machine. It arrived five days later, the same day that I picked my first harvest of portobello mushrooms. They were as big, if not an even bigger success than the oyster mushrooms. Had they not seen me prepare them with the same spices as the warbull, they wouldn't have believed they weren't actually eating some sort of steak.

However, even that didn't convince the other clans to start producing some of their own. It created this really awkward situation where our neighbors wanted to trade for my mushrooms. But clans didn't normally trade on that scale with an individual. Since every clan acted almost as a single organism, with everyone pooling their resources, in our case, it could have been trading mushrooms for ore with the Inosh Mountain Clan, or for polished stones from the White River Clan, etc. However, my vegetables were considered my personal property as I had 'individually crafted them' like any jewel or weapon a Crafter created was his or hers to reap the benefits of.

I eventually worked it out with them crafting fancy containers, baskets, wrapping cloths and papers for my jams, berries, and the other goods I started adding to the roster based on demand. To my shock, when I suggested that a long-term trade that would definitely help me would be compost, instead of getting brutally shut down for trying to con them into dirt digging chores, I got an enthusiastic response from all the clans.

Living close to nature, the Andturians were very environmentally conscientious, despite their limited understanding of responsible farming of the land. The Andturians naturally composted all of their organic wastes which they eventually disposed of in their fields. Between their compost and all the manure from their mraka herd, my needs for natural fertilizers were met.

The month following that first market was magical. Olix and I spent a great deal of time together, getting to know each other. As much as the mraka had initially traumatized me, I was growing more and more comfortable riding one on my own with that crazy saddle Kayog had given us. For now, Olix was only making me ride around open fields, while showing me the nearby landmarks and the general beauty of his world.

I was falling in love with Xecania, the Andturians, and their easy way of life. That play day, we'd ridden our beasts to a particular field that took my breath away. Lush, yellowish green grass spread as far as the eye could see beneath the bluest of skies where the three moons of my new homeworld hung low. A flock of birds was performing acrobatics above us in a mesmerizing dance. We dismounted and sat directly on the grass for a while to rest from riding the mrakas.

Olix talked about his youth, and how much time he'd spent here.

"Zoltar and I often came to this specific field to hunt moshins. They are furry little creatures that greatly resemble your rabbits but with flat tails and short, round ears," Olix explained in light of my confused expression. "Ever since we could walk, my cousin and I knew we would be Hunters, just like Luped knew she would be a Builder. It is like a calling in our blood."

Sitting between his legs, my back resting on his chest, I was slowly tracing the pattern of the scales on his tail, which he had recurved over my lap. Olix had taken to doing that often whenever he held or hugged me, embracing me with his tail as well in a way that felt wonderfully possessive. It was like he wished he had an extra pair of arms to keep me close and make sure I never went away.

I tilted my head to look up at him. "Do you still hunt here?" I asked.

He nodded. "Yes, but rarely. We usually leave this field for the young to practice their hunting skills. It is a safe area, and it teaches them to coordinate their strategy, work on their speed, and learn to adapt to the escape pattern of their prey," Olix said, excitement seeping into his voice. "We will bring the young here next week for play day, but not to actually catch anything. We will use a holographic simulation Luped has been working on. While moshins reproduce quickly, we do not want to put a strain on their population by hunting them too aggressively."

"That's really cool," I said, once more struck by the extent of my husband's passion for hunting. He would never feel such a passion for what I did. "So, all the children get to pick their profession?"

"Yes, although their calling usually manifests itself early on," Olix explained. "By the time they are three or four, we usually know what they will want to do."

"But…" I hesitated, choosing my words carefully, as I looked back at his tail to hide my expression. "Has a child ever been forced to go on a different path than the one that called to them?"

"No," he replied without hesitation. His embrace tightened around me, and he gently brushed his cheek against my hair before plopping a kiss on top of my head. "You are thinking about Nosha."

My head jerked back towards him, studying his features. To

my relief, there was no anger or accusation there. I nodded, bracing for what he would say.

"Her parents are distressed by her fascination with your farming activities," Olix confessed, matter-of-factly. "We all assumed she would be a Gatherer, like her grandfather Pawis. But since your arrival, she's become obsessed with growing things."

"I haven't encouraged or incentivized her in any way," I quickly replied.

Olix smiled, caressed my cheek, then leaned down to kiss my lips. "I know, my mate. We are all aware of it and are grateful you haven't tried to influence her," he said in a reassuring voice. "Continue as you are until her parents tell you otherwise. If the Spirits have decided that this should be her calling, then so it shall be. For now, she's still very young and will be trained as a Gatherer. In three years, when Nosha turns seven, it will be her decision, and the people will honor it."

I sighed with relief. Nosha was an adorable little girl who had been all but shadowing me from a distance since the day I'd transplanted my first sprouts. A number of times, I'd caught her carefully walking between the rows to observe, not disturbing anything. She'd been particularly fascinated by my watering and weeding machines. Since I'd acquired my upgraded model after the last public market, she'd been even more mesmerized. Nosha had the flame in her. I'd kill to be able to nurture it.

"I know we've never talked about kids yet, but what will happen with ours?" I asked carefully. "I know they will 100% look Andturian, but I would want to pass on part of my heritage to my children."

This time, Olix made me turn around to face him, sitting on his lap, with my legs on each side of him. His large hands gently caressed my back while he stared me in the eye.

"Our offspring will know about both our cultures," Olix pledged. "If they show a natural desire to learn your trade, I will not stand in their way. Every clan member has the right to choose their destiny and to thrive according to the path the Spirits have laid out for them."

"Even though your people have a low opinion of my trade?" I insisted.

"My people hate what farming was under the invaders," Olix explained. "You are showing it to us under a completely different light. It will take time, but mentalities will evolve. That said, remember that Andturians were *never* farmers, even before the Vaengi came here. It was never a calling for us. Some people grew a few things, more as a hobby than anything else, and we also grew spices. I know what you keep hoping in your heart, but you are only setting yourself up for disappointment. Only the Spirits know what future generations will do. But for now—"

A beep on my com startled us. Although I always carried it with me, I hardly ever got any calls, except from Luped telling me to get out of my shed and come eat, or to come see the advancement of my new greenhouse or of the shop.

The message on the screen made me frown.

"What is it?" Olix asked.

"It's from your mother. A human from the Conglomerate just showed up at the shop," I said, tension oozing out of my voice. "I bet he's pissed about the complaint Luped and I filed."

"Probably," Olix replied, his face hardening in a way that was both frightening and strangely sexy. "Let's go greet him."

My husband was always even-tempered and gentle, but a predator lurked beneath his sweet demeanor. I couldn't help but find that to be quite the turn on. Olix got up, holding me before setting me on my feet. We hurried to our mrakas—my man helping me onto the back of mine that was way too high—then raced back home.

A little less than ten minutes later, we reached the village. A shiny, top-of-the-line, personal shuttle with a massive logo of the Conglomerate sat on our landing pad. To my surprise, a gorgeous human male waited for us by the entrance of the shop. A number of villagers had gathered around, staring him down. The man looked completely unfazed, shrouded in a veil of self-right-eousness and overconfidence that made me uneasy. I didn't doubt for a minute he was here to bully us.

Olix hopped down from his mraka, before the beast even came to a full stop, with a deftness and grace that made my chest swell with pride. For the first time, I was truly seeing the predator in my husband. His muscles rolled beneath his shiny scales as he prowled towards me to help me down, although his gaze remained locked on the human. The slow swaying of his tail reminded me of an ominous pendulum, ticking down to the moment Olix would unleash his beast.

It was sexy as all hell.

After he put me on my feet, I took my husband's hand, and we approached the intruder. The obvious relief from our clan hinted that things had been getting heated. The man observed us as we closed the distance with him. His gaze lingered on our clasped hands, his face unreadable as he gave my mate an assessing once over, before turning back to me.

"Ms. Jennings, I'm glad you were able to come so quickly," he said with a seductive smile. "My name is David Lord, Divi-sion Director with the Conglomerate. But please call me David."

Under different circumstances, I'd probably be drooling before this hot piece of a man. Tall, the right level of muscular, polished appearance, the face of an angel with the sinful smile of a sex god, and the type of sexy, manly voice that would have any woman's girly bits stand to attention, he likely left a trail of exploded ovaries on his path wherever he went... except here.

"Hello, Mr. Lord," I said, ignoring his request. "Jennings is my maiden's name. It's Mrs. Nillis now. And this is my husband, Olix Nillis, Clan Leader of the Monkoo tribe."

Although his plush lips stretched into an apologetic smile, I didn't miss the slight hardening of his stunning hazel eyes.

"I stand corrected, *Mrs.* Nillis," he replied.

"What are you doing on our lands, Mr. Lord?" Olix asked.

"I'm here to discuss the disloyal practices here at your village," the male said, gesturing at the store with his head, "as well as some defamatory comments and inaccurate claims filed against us by your wife, who no doubt doesn't realize her misunderstanding of the laws," Mr. Lord added, in a patronizing tone that made me want to punch him in the throat. "The Conglomerate wants to file a lawsuit against Ms. Jennings… apologies, Mrs. Nillis, but I asked them to stay any procedures until I had a chance to discuss the matter with your mate and your people. As you can guess, these can get extremely costly."

That fucking snake! His words had on the clan the exact effect he'd been hoping for. The last market had given us some breathing room. But a costly trial would destroy all that we had achieved or hoped to accomplish in the future.

But his words didn't work on my husband or me.

"I dare them to sue us," Olix replied, taking a threatening step towards Mr. Lord.

CHAPTER 17
OLIX

My blood boiled with barely repressed rage. How dare they send their puppet to threaten my mate and my people? They'd never sent a human before. I'd watched enough sexual videos with my Susan to know that David Lord matched the type of males human females were drawn to. The way he'd looked at and spoken to my mate made no mystery he was trying to seduce her. But she'd put him back in his place, claimed my name as hers, and clearly established she was mine. While pride swelled within me, fury almost superseded it.

Most off-worlder species considered us as inferior. They viewed us as primitive from both a societal and technological standpoint. The barely veiled condescension hidden behind obnoxious smiles made my claws itch with the need to lacerate their faces.

"No illegal business is being run here, and no defamatory or false claims were filed against your Conglomerate," I said forcefully.

In this instant, I felt more grateful than ever that my female and sister had thoroughly informed me of all the steps they had taken when filing against the Conglomerate. My Susan had further spent time with me going over the various laws protecting our people, and lands and all the recourses we could take against offenders.

In the past, it had been so overwhelming to navigate on our own. Even my mate had gotten some headaches sorting some of these things out. But she'd cleverly reached out to Kayog, who had put us in touch with a lawyer of the United Planets Organization to validate our assumptions.

"We are the native people of this planet," I hissed at the man. "We do not need permission to run any kind of commerce on our lands. My Susan is Andturian through her marriage to me. But even without that, as long as *we* authorize it, any business can operate on our lands. The rest of *you* are limited to the public market, the spaceport, or the resort shops."

The human scoffed, as if I'd said something ludicrous. "Whoever gave you that silly idea?" he asked, casting a meaningful glance towards my mate. "That's not how it works, Clan Leader," the intruder continued, stating my title with an underlying hint of mockery. "All business is regulated under the same laws."

"All *off-worlder* business is regulated under Law E75 of the UPO Prime Act," I retorted with disdain.

I made no effort to repress my smug smile when he failed to hide his initial shock before regaining his composure. My Susan squeezing my hand with pride only pumped me up further. Knowledge was power. I hadn't known these things before, which had allowed them to bully us. We'd tried to learn more but had always felt overwhelmed with the legal language in Universal and without the guidance of someone who knew more. In the less than two months she'd been with us, my Susan had made my knowledge and understanding grow by leaps and bounds, stopped me from feeling so helpless, and helped me gain the confidence to face the future in these changing times.

"You are forbidden from running businesses anywhere

outside of the resorts and spaceport without the express consent of a native species," I continued, my voice loud and clear for my people to hear as well. "And such businesses may not directly compete with native trade in a disloyal fashion. Your Conglomerate has deliberately misled tourists and customers with your fake and cheap replicas of our goods, and yet labeled them "Authentic, hand-made, Andturian" products in direct violation of Articles 4 through 12 of Law E75."

"We did no such things!" Mr. Lord said, losing some of his confidence.

"You most certainly did," my mate countered. "I saw it first-hand—and took pictures—in the souvenir shops at the spaceport. We also have countless testimonies from the residents of the Bosengi villages as well as from the tourist resorts. And it's not just a complaint that was filed, we're also suing for all those violations, disloyal competition, and exemplary damages."

"You think throwing around a series of laws and articles are going to threaten us?" the human male said, going on the offensive. "You have no idea who you are going after. Our pockets are endless, yours not so much, little girl. Your *husband* there," he said with contempt while glancing at me, "is on the verge of bankruptcy and of his people starving to death. Even if we let you have the exclusive market to sell your little trinkets, it will never be enough to feed five clans. You playing farm won't help either. They are first and foremost carnivores. Hard to eat when there is no game to be found."

"And you wouldn't happen to have any idea what's been driving away the herds, would you?" Susan snapped, glaring at the man.

"Why would I know anything about it? Do I look like a woodsman to you?" he asked haughtily.

"We have always provided for our clans," I snarled. "Even with the thinning herds, there are other ways for us to acquire meat."

"You mean trading the credits you earn by selling trinkets?" the human said with a gleeful malice. "We set the prices for the imported meat being sold on this planet. Making enemies out of us isn't very smart. You will want to think about that before your lawsuit goes to trial."

"Is that a threat?" I asked menacingly.

"I'm merely stating facts. Do with them what you will," he replied with a dismissive gesture. "We tried to be reasonable with you people, we made you generous offers and negotiated in good faith. In response, you are attacking us just so that you can hang on to the most fertile lands in the solar system. But why? You're letting them go to waste while countless planets are struggling with hunger."

"If interplanetary hunger and good faith negotiations had been your goal, you would have proposed alternatives, such as renting their lands for farming," Susan interjected. "But you didn't offer that because this is about fattening your wallets. Renting would subject you to too many ethical and best practice rules that would affect your bottom line. You're like a swarm of locusts. You want to acquire these lands, exploit them until the soil and local environment is exhausted and ruined, and then you'll move on to greener pastures. It's not going to happen here."

David Lord shook his head at my mate with disdain and then at me with pity. It took every ounce of my willpower not to beat him into a pulp.

"This woman will be your ruin," he said with false empathy. "I tried to reason with you, but as you will clearly not budge, I have no choice but to proceed with the Board's decision. As of this instant, the price offered by the Conglomerate for your lands has been reduced by 15%. And that price will continue to go down by 5% every week."

"Spare yourself the trouble of revising it every week," I said with contempt. "I've said no before, and that will never change.

As for your lawsuit, bring it on. Our lawyer from the UPO is eagerly awaiting to have a conversation with yours. Now, get the fuck off my lands before I throw you out. And don't ever show your face here again."

The human's face visibly grew paler. I'd never seen this on my mate. But considering the fearful expression that flashed over his features, I was glad my Susan had never blanched like this. Mr. Lord opened and closed his mouth a couple of times, as if trying to find a good, stinging reply but gave up. After one final glare at my female, he turned on his heels, and hastily marched to his shuttle.

We stared at him until his shuttle took off and became a small dot on the horizon.

"You totally kicked ass," my mate said, hugging me.

"Only thanks to you, my Susan," I said, my heart swelling with the growing affection she stirred in me. "Without your guidance and insights, he might have fooled us."

"He can't harm us?" Kuani asked timidly behind us.

I turned around to look at my clan. The same uncertainty and worry could be read on all of their faces.

"No, he cannot," I said reassuringly. "Those threats are meant to frighten us into submitting to their will. Everyone, gather at the Great Hall. Round up the ones still off on play day. We will tell you what my Susan, Luped, and I have been working on to put an end to the Conglomerate's abuse."

It took a bit of time to gather everyone. Then, for nearly an hour, the three of us gave extensive details to the clan of the legal steps we had been taking and why we felt confident they couldn't harm us. It was incredibly empowering to have answers and to feel competent giving them. Our people felt it, and their worry not only evaporated, but their admiration grew. As much as my clan loved me, my leadership had been increasingly questioned since the beginning of our troubles. But it now felt stronger than ever, thanks to my delicate wisp of a mate.

It didn't solve our meat problem. The human had struck a nerve with his comment about the scarcity of game and the fact that they could regulate the price of the meat sold on their markets. It had been one of our backup plans, although not the first. Thankfully, we still had more time before that potentially became a problem.

When the meeting ended and the people scattered, we sent messages to the other four clan leaders to warn them of what had happened in case Mr. Lord tried to bully them as well. As a matter of fact, the dirty worm had arrived just moments prior at the Inosh Mountains Clan, making the same threat about the reduced offer for the lands. The Conglomerate had been hammering hard on Surtas. That they knew his clan hurt the most only reinforced my belief that they were somehow involved in the vanishing herds. But we simply couldn't find proof of their wrongdoing, and especially not how they were doing it.

However, Surtas was in awe of my mate. He believed she'd been personally anointed by the Spirits themselves and then sent to us. As we'd kept the other clan leaders apprised of our legal efforts, he wasn't taken unawares by Mr. Lord's comments. Surtas gladly kicked the human out of his lands with the same threat of not coming back.

Now, we only needed to make sure we continued to find ways to thrive. Business at my Susan's store had exploded in the three weeks after the public market. She was selling out on both days the store was open per week. Some of the Gatherers that mostly took care of cooking were showing growing interest in preparing some of the cooked products my Susan had begun selling or was considering to. But we couldn't depend on my female's work to keep us afloat.

"Honey, do you have a minute?"

Susan's voice pulled me out of my musing. She'd taken to giving me all kinds of strange names. It had thrown me for a loop at first before she explained they were affectionate names humans gave people they loved. It did something funny to me to hear her say that word. My female wasn't in love with me, but the tenderness, respect, and deep friendship that kept growing between us was undeniably leading us there. It didn't hurt that we had incredible passion and chemistry on top of it.

Still, honey was a strange name. I liked its sweet and soothing connotation, but it seemed awkwardly mild for an apex Hunter such as I.

"Yes, my mate," I said, sitting on one of the benches in the Great Hall and pulling her onto my lap. "Before we got interrupted, this afternoon was supposed to be just you and me."

She smiled and caressed my cheek. "When that idiot was talking shit, I suddenly got an idea that I wanted to run past you."

"I'm listening," I replied, my curiosity piqued.

"You know how I feel about all of these great farmlands going to waste," she said carefully. I nodded. "When I told him that if he'd been genuine about good faith negotiations, he could have offered to rent your lands to farm them. Do you remember that?"

I nodded again, this time with a slight frown.

"Wait! Don't freak out yet," she exclaimed preemptively, guessing by my expression that I wasn't too keen on where I thought this conversation was headed. "I will never be in favor of anything that would make the clans lose control in whole or in part of the lands, even if only for a predefined amount of time. But this is our biggest wealth. And that idiot is right: there are many overpopulated planets out there—or others with difficult climates—that could really use the massive amounts of food we could produce here."

"We're not farmers, Susan," I said, a sliver of anger seeping into my voice. "You will not convert the clans. I thought that matter had been settled, and that you understood that now."

"I do! I promise you, I do!" she said in an appeasing tone. "I'm not trying to convert them. Please, let me finish."

Still confused and slightly irritated, I nodded, forcing myself to keep an open mind.

"Based on the way the clan has been reacting to me working the fields, they don't seem to have a problem with people farming using modern methods that aren't backbreaking and that are both safe and respectful to the environment. It is just not something that they are personally ready and willing to do. Correct?"

I nodded. "Yes, that is correct."

"So, why don't we just hire people to work the farms?" Susan asked. "We pay them respectable wages, provide them with lodging, that will all be covered by the proceeds we will make selling the crops off world. I already know a list of serious buyers that would be all too eager to do business with us. And even better, if we failed to fix the disappearing herd issue, we could negotiate some straight up trades of our products for their meat. These lands are perfect to grow wheat that we can transform into flour. Flour is always in huge demand. We'd have no problem finding people to trade us good quality meat for it."

I gaped at Susan, a million thoughts running through my mind. Although I hated the possibility that hunting might become obsolete, ensuring the prosperity of our clans had to be my main priority.

"But who would we hire?" I asked, refusing to allow myself to get carried away by enthusiasm. "Xecania is considered far too primitive by most species. The ultra-rich come here as tourists to brag about buying baubles from savages," I added in self-derision. "No one else will want to come here where everything still needs to be built. And even if we find people, how can we be sure they aren't going to be a threat to our way of life? Like all of the other natives, we are a peaceful species. We don't lock our doors. We don't have defensive walls, or—"

"And we wouldn't need any," Susan interrupted, her eyes sparkling with excitement. "There are plenty of people who will want to come here. The right people. People like me, with a passion and expertise in farming, but with nowhere to call home."

My eyes widened as understanding dawned on me.

"Third daughters of Meterion," I whispered.

"Yes!" Susan said with a grin. "Most of us never get chosen when we try to get matched through mating agencies because we have nothing but ourselves, our skills, and our passion for working the land. If you hadn't accepted me, I'd be breaking my back slaving away under terrible conditions in a factory in the city, or as a servant to some asshole. If a chance like this had been offered to me, I would have absolutely taken it over mating a stranger."

I nodded slowly, my heart soaring at the incredible opportunities this presented. "But you are unique, my Susan," I argued, still cautious. "Assuming other third daughters are indeed interested in coming here, how do we know their personalities will be compatible with our people and lifestyle?"

"Kayog!" Susan said smugly, as if that was self-evident. "The minute he talked to me, he knew you and I would be a great match. We can retain his services to interview the interested candidates and forward to us the ones that his empathic abilities judge adequate."

"That is brilliant," I said, staring at my mate in awe. "You have thought of everything!"

"Hardly," she said, puffing out her chest. "It's just been simmering in my mind for the past two hours since shit-face left. I'm sure there's a bunch of things I haven't thought of yet, but I think this could be a solid plan."

I chuckled, pleased far more than I would ever admit by all the derogatory words my Susan used to describe the far too pretty human that had come to bully us. I'd never been the jealous type, but I couldn't bear the thought of my female looking at another male the way she looked at me.

"You are truly a wonder, my Susan," I said with affection. "Let us discuss this further with Luped and Kayog to see how feasible this would be. They will require work permits, transportation, and lodging. Once here, they may not wish to live according to Andturian culture. In which case, they will need their own little village with the standard amenities humans require, among other things."

She nodded, not daunted in the least by the amount of work this would involve.

"Once we have a clearer picture, we can present your idea to the clans and hold a vote," I said.

"Sounds like a plan," Susan said, beaming at me.

"You are my blessing from the Spirits," I whispered before kissing her.

CHAPTER 18
SUSAN

To Olix's utter dismay, my period struck the following day, nine days before the next public market. Although I'd warned him of it beforehand, the poor man was a total wreck. I've always had a heavy flow, occasionally accompanied by nasty cramps and head-splitting migraines. I therefore couldn't blame him for sneaking Molzeg into my room every time I'd go curl up in our bed so that she could make sure I wasn't bleeding to death.

I couldn't even get mad, he was so distressed.

My husband was such a cuddly teddy bear. He would massage my back and my legs to soothe some of the cramps, and my feet to help me relax—all based on videos he'd watched on the topic. I could already imagine what kind of mother hen he would be the day I became pregnant.

Even though we still had four months to go in our trial period, I already knew I wasn't going anywhere. Olix was the perfect partner I couldn't even have invented for myself. I was falling in love with him, and he was becoming my best friend. But our cultural differences continued to both make me chuckle and want to pull my hair out.

While he was beside himself with joy when my period finally ended after six days, he refused to touch me for another two days, fearing he might make me bleed again. Even though I'd explained the science behind it all, he wouldn't accept that my body wasn't low on blood reserves. Instead, he made it a point to feed me to bursting to rebuild my strength.

Sigh. I couldn't get mad at that either.

On the third day, I lay down in the center of our bed. As soon as I heard him approaching our bedroom, I held a tablet in one hand while watching some porn at maximum volume, and started masturbating, my legs spread facing the door. When he asked me what I was doing, I very seriously answered that since my husband had lost all desire for me, I had no choice but to take care of myself. That night, I got thoroughly fucked by my man who was offended I would dare think he no longer wanted me.

Success!

On the eve of the next market, our lawyer informed us the charges the Conglomerate had brought against us had been dropped. Although they pulled all of their 'Andturian' products from the souvenir shops in both the spaceport and the tourist resorts, we didn't drop our own complaints and lawsuits. Until the future of our clans was secured, and so long as the threat of the Conglomerate persisted, we wouldn't give an inch.

The best part was that, thanks to our protected Prime species status, the United Planets Organization provided us with free legal services. No wonder the Conglomerate had pulled their lawsuits. They'd go bankrupt before the UPO on those litigations. Still, they hadn't offered to settle with us on our own lawsuits. I had no doubt it was to avoid giving us a large chunk of money that would make us immune from their pressure for us to sell them our lands.

The following market also turned out to be a success, a better one even than the previous month. With the Conglomerate's goods no longer competing with ours, plenty of tourists flocked to our Crafters' stalls, their sales further aided by my so-called discounts.

For the reezia berries, I'd always wanted 50 marks a basket for myself, but had planned on bumping the price to 60 marks to cover the cost of the crafted items. When that Bosengi female had offered 60 right off the bat, I'd just gotten ballsy and asked for 70 instead. I'd nearly fainted when she'd agreed. So, there was no discount. They were paying full-price for everything, with a 10-mark bonus per basket for yours truly when bought individually instead of as a rack.

With the proceeds from that market sales and the ones I'd been accumulating over the past month from my store, I was able to buy a small personal shuttle. It could only carry four passengers and a small cargo, but it finally allowed us to go visit the other native species and come back home the same day.

Life was good.

It got even better when, three days after the market, Kayog confirmed that he could not only handle the job posting and coordinate the interviews on Meterion for us, he would also manage the relocation of the women, all of it free of charge for us. It turned out that, even though these were not marriage-based matches, it was still matchmaking for a Prime planet with someone that could help the development of Xecania. Therefore, the UPO would cover his fees.

I could have kissed that Temern. In many ways, Kayog was our fairy godfather.

With much apprehension, Olix and I presented the project of hiring third daughters from Meterion to work our fields. I nearly wept at the open-minded reaction of the clan. Like my husband, they bombarded us with questions for which we had all the answers, thanks to Olix's foresight that we be thoroughly prepared first. While certain things still needed to be decided by the clan—like which of the locations we had proposed would serve as the human village—the project was unanimously approved.

The way a few of the males eyed my virgin blood still adorning my husband's weapons and accessories, I suspected the single ones were wondering at the possibility of scoring themselves a virgin as well. I barely refrained from rolling my eyes. I didn't know that any of those women would be interested in a relationship with an Andturian. Frankly, if not for my desperate situation, I wouldn't have considered it. But once they started mingling with the people on a regular basis as they came to work here, things could change.

Time would tell.

Using my spiffy little shuttle, Olix, Luped, and I traveled to the other four clans to present our project, with the same positive result.

I was flying high, literally and figuratively. I hadn't converted my new people to farming but, thanks to my expertise, I'd helped ensure a prosperous future for them and the children Olix and I would have. I wanted Xecania to be the next Meterion, but even better.

With the end of the first week of the month approaching, my heart constricted at the thought of Olix and half of the clan leaving for another great hunt and fishing expedition. The past five weeks with my husband by my side had been magical. I hated the thought that he'd be gone for two to three weeks. But that couldn't be helped. Our meat reserves were running low, and the Conglomerate had indeed steadily increased the price of its imported meats. But they were a last resort. If it came to that, the plan was to purchase meat from the other native species whose hunting territories hadn't been impacted like ours.

Funny enough, those species didn't have farming lands. Coincidence?

With my first batch of beets, potatoes, squash, and tomatoes, I wanted to make the clan a special meal before their departure.

As I wanted to include a few Andturian ingredients, I joined the Gathering expedition that was off to pick some jovam roots, among other things. With the clan's blessing, I would now grow them as well in my field, so they no longer had to be this parsimonious in consuming them.

While I'd visited the forest since my arrival on Xecania, I'd never gone very deep into it. The handful of times we had—at my insistence—Olix had fairly quickly turned us around to show me other wonders of his homeworld. That had struck me as slightly strange. But I figured that, as a Hunter, he'd spent so much time in the forest struggling to find game of late, that it reminded him of the difficulties that plagued the clans. Anyway, his world had plenty of other things that would blow me away.

As I loved nature, this walk in the forest was a triple treat for me. On top of the promenade, I would get to see how the Gatherers chose which roots were ripe—including the proper method to extract them—but also the kind of soil and environment they grew in. Unlike the Bosengi berries and vegetables I had been growing for my store, there were no guidelines on growing jovam roots. I would have to go based on observation of their environment and the pH of the soil, among other things.

There were twenty of us, traipsing through the forest, little Nosha flanking me. She was so adorable, it took all my willpower not to pick her up and cover her lovely face with kisses. Seeing her and the couple other kids that had joined us made me ache for a child of my own. Truth be told, I'd been disappointed when my period had come. Olix and I had been *extremely* active sexually over the past five weeks. I'd been so sure we would have conceived. And yet…

Pawis headed towards one of the large aldomyan trees filling the forest. They were fairly spaced out, which made sense considering the size of the trunk and massive roots that spread deep and wide. Looking at the dark, almost black bark with dark red veins in the grooves, and their long, spiraling branches with wide, brownish red leaves made me feel like I'd walked into a whimsical world. A few different types of trees were interspersed among them, their trunks almost the same dark color, but their leaves a purplish blue or midnight blue hue. Oddly, while few of their tree leaves bore the standard green I was used to, the forest floor was covered in a large amount of greeneries, from very pale green to super dark.

It was among those patches of greens in the underbrush that Pawis began harvesting the root using some kind of trowel to loosen the earth around it. It took me no time to recognize the type of leaves that belonged to the jovam roots.

"The length and size of their leaves is how you know they are ready to harvest," Pawis explained while picking another large root. "Try it," he said, giving me his trowel.

I gladly proceeded, choosing one of the roots and stabbing at the packed earth around it with the tool to loosen it. The elder Gatherer's eyes lit with mirth when it took me a few attempts, and then I struggled to pull the root out, even by putting my back into it. When I managed to yank it out, I stumbled a couple of steps back, which earned me a few giggles from Nosha and a handful of Gatherers nearby. Strength-wise, I would never compare with these guys. I made faces at them, which only made them laugh more before they got back to work.

I gave Pawis his trowel back and whipped out my portable analyzer to study the soil. With the large quantity of ripe jovam roots I could see just in this area, we would have a really nice haul today. While waiting for the analyzer to perform its magic, I gazed at my companions working methodically and efficiently, even little Nosha put me to shame with the ease with which she harvested a few roots.

Oddly, the upbeat atmosphere we'd started out with dampened relatively quickly. The happy chatter that always provided a lively buzz around the Andturians, whether when crafting on the plaza or cooking inside the Great Hall, had died down. Every face had taken on a serious expression—if not to say sullen—as they continued to work.

Glancing around me, I realized my companions were starting to move away from our current location, leaving a lot of mature roots behind. Pawis scrunched his face, his nose twitching. He stared for a second at the patch of roots in front of him, many of which were beyond ready to be harvested, but he turned around, his lizard eyes flicking this way and that as if looking for a new place to harvest. His nose twitched again, and he moved away, looking mildly irritated.

Although confused, I shrugged and went back to my work, taking a few shots of the other type of plants surrounding the roots—none of which I recognized—but that I intended to research once we got back home. That's when I spotted a dark, gelatinous growth on some of the thick, gnarly roots of the trees and their bark. They almost blended with the trees, making them very hard to spot.

I squealed, rushing towards one of them, wanting to make sure my eyes weren't fooling me. Alerted by my scream, a few of the Gatherers—that had begun wandering farther from my current location—came back to check up on me, a worried expression on their faces.

"What is that?" I asked Junit, a young male in his early twenties. "It looks like the wood ear mushrooms that humans eat. They are *delicious*!"

Junit scrunched his face, his nose twitching the way Pawis's had previously.

"No," he said, shaking his head. "This is a pest, a bad fungus on the trees. We don't eat that. Stay away from it," the male responded in an unusually clipped tone.

Without giving me a chance to respond, he turned on his heels and swiftly walked away. The handful of other Gatherers that had come to investigate gave me a stern look before leaving as well.

What the fuck just happened?

Baffled, I looked back at the fungus. Upon closer inspection, although it did look like wood ears color-wise, the shape was closer to snow fungus and the edges had a thin red fur that seemed to produce spores. I took a few pictures and brushed some of the spores to stick them in my analyzer. While waiting for the results, I headed towards my companions whose behavior was becoming stranger by the minute. They were now walking past entire patches of jovam roots, not appearing to see them or deliberately ignoring them. Nosha was standing in the middle of the small clearing, looking a little confused as she absent-mindedly rubbed her nose with the back of her hand.

"Pawis," I called out, when I found the elder Gatherer just standing in the middle of the forest, staring blindly at the ground. "Pawis!" I called out again, louder, when he failed to respond.

His head jerked towards me. Eyes glassy, nose twitching, he appeared to struggle to emerge from whatever daydream he was falling into.

Something is affecting them.

"I guess that is all for today," Pawis said in a disappointed voice. "It started out well. I had hope for a bigger harvest, but there aren't enough that are ripe just yet. Let's go home."

Everyone nodded, many appearing relieved.

I gaped at them in disbelief as they hastily started to make their way back home. All around us, the plush leaves of tons of mature roots—some even looking like they would soon be overly ripe—were gently swaying in the breeze. I took pictures of the roots the Gatherers had left behind. Moments later, my analyzer beeped to announce it had completed its work, startling me. I didn't need to read it to know what the results would say. A glance confirmed my suspicion: powerful hallucinogen.

Instead of the jovam root samples that I had intended to bring back to use as starter seed for my crops, I collected a few dark mushrooms. By the time I placed the fourth one in my bag, my nose was starting to itch, and a slightly nauseous feeling had settled in the pit of my stomach. A mild pressure at the back of my head hinted at a possible incoming monster headache.

Not dallying any further, I hurried after my companions.

By the time we exited the forest, the itching in my nose had receded, like the ill sensations that had started creeping up on me. The same was happening to the rest of the Gatherers whose sour mood had just as abruptly lifted, their more jovial demeanor gradually resurfacing, despite their disappointment at our poor harvest.

I made a beeline for my husband. He was working at one of the forges, Zoltar, and a handful of other Hunters and Crafters nearby, also working on preparing their weapons and nets for the upcoming great hunt and fishing expedition.

"Olix, we need to talk," I said in an urgent voice.

All eyes turned towards me, my tone stirring curiosity and worry among the nearby clanmates.

"What is wrong, my Susan?" Olix asked, putting down the mold he had been making arrowheads in. "Did something happen during the Gathering?"

"Yes," I said, my voice tense with a strange mix of anger and excitement. "There's a hallucinogenic mushroom in your forest that's messing with people's heads. And I'm wondering if it could also be messing with the herds."

A general gasp rose around me, shock and hope descending on every face. A part of me wondered if it had been a mistake to speak of my suspicions in front of everyone instead of using my husband's methodical approach of getting all the answers first. But they would be leaving on a great hunt in the next couple of days. There wasn't enough time for Olix, Luped, and me to investigate. The more people on this, the faster we would get solid answers.

"Explain, my mate," Olix asked, taking a step closer to me.

Realizing something big was happening, the Crafters stopped

their work, and everyone approached us, including the Gatherers that had just returned from the forest with me. I gestured at Kuani's worktable, asking permission to use part of it. The female nodded, moving aside some of the housewares she'd been working on. I placed my sample bag on the table, opened the flap so that it would lie down on the surface, then drew out a couple of dark mushrooms. I left them sitting on the flap so as to not contaminate Kuani's workspace.

The Andturians recoiled, many muttering about why I would bring this rot to the village.

"I believe this is the source of all your problems," I said, pointing at the mushroom.

I recounted what I had just witnessed. Pawis and Junit gaped at me in shock, not recalling having any such behavior, nor did the others.

"And you wouldn't because the hallucinogens were messing with your heads," I said sympathetically. "Look at the people closest to the mushroom," I added, pointing at them. "Their noses are already starting to twitch, and I bet you all want to get away from here."

They nodded, flabbergasted. I placed the mushrooms back inside the bag and closed the flap, not wanting to needlessly indispose them.

"That's the behavior I witnessed," I continued. "I took pictures of the patches of jovam that the Gatherers all walked away from earlier, saying there was nothing left to harvest."

I passed Pawis my tablet, and the poor male stared at the images in shock. He handed the tablet over to the other Gatherers and members of the clan for all of them to see, then grabbed his quills at the back of his head with both hands, distress and disbelief warring on his face.

"So many roots going to waste, rotting in the ground," he whispered, floored.

"You couldn't see it," I said in an appeasing voice. "As soon as we left the forest, you all returned to your normal, charming selves. You did nothing wrong. It's a good thing we left when we did because the spores were starting to affect me, too. Who knows what a mess I might have been then?"

"But why did it take longer with you?" Zoltar asked, with genuine confusion.

"I think it's because the Andturian nose is more sensitive than a human's," I replied pensively. "Therefore, I needed to be exposed to the spores a lot longer before they started affecting me. There might be other reasons but, even though our noses are pretty long, our sense of smell isn't that developed," I said in self-derision.

That earned me a few amused smiles. The Andturians some-times teased me for my unusual features, but never in a mean or hurtful way. To them, my nose made them think that someone had tried to steal it out of my face, but it was too well-attached, so it just remained pointy when the would-be thief gave up.

"You know," Pawis said, looking like he'd just been struck by a new idea, "it's been a little over a year since I've noticed the first one of these mushrooms. There weren't that many back then."

"I bet if we ask Surtas about these mushrooms, he will say they've been around for about two years," Olix said, anger descending on his features.

Zoltar emitted a rattling hiss that spoke of fury, echoed by many of the others.

"The same time those vermin from the Conglomerate started putting pressure on us to sell our lands," Zoltar said between his teeth.

I nodded. "That would be a very clever way to drive you out without getting caught," I said, anger bubbling inside of me. "But we can't just throw around accusations," I cautioned them. "I genuinely believe this is what is driving away the herds. Judging by the basic analysis my device made of the spores, it's an airborne hallucinogen that would affect pretty much any air-breathing species. It is abnormal that we didn't encounter a single animal in the forest. There's always life in some form, little scurrying creatures in the underbrush, others climbing and nesting in the trees. Even the birds were nowhere to be found except very high up near the tree line, away from the spores."

"We had noticed," Olix said. "We figured the same thing happening to the herds was driving away the smaller creatures. Now we know. Time to eradicate this rot."

"We have the filtration masks we use when mining," said Tokus—one of the wood and ore Gatherers. "We could use them to remove the rot and harvest the jovam roots."

It was a clever temporary idea until we found a proper and permanent way of eradicating its propagation. We burst into action, everyone spreading while Olix and I contacted the other clans to inform them of my discovery.

EPILOGUE
SUSAN

An entire day spent removing the mushrooms and burning them proved our test conclusive. Obviously, we hadn't covered the entire forest—it was much too vast. But in the large areas that were cleared, life started creeping back in over the following days. The Gatherers were also able to walk about mask-less without being negatively affected.

The Inosh Mountains region was riddled with the mushrooms, clearly indicating the spread had begun there. Each clan brought samples from their respective region, which I submitted to the UPO representative of their Prime Planets Health and Environmental Service. As we suspected, the mushroom was not only a foreign organism introduced to Xecania's ecosystem, it had been genetically modified. An analysis of the spread pattern confirmed it had been deliberately implanted in strategic locations on the planet.

The problem was that the wind, water, insects, and the animals that had previously dwelled in those areas, had carried the spores a much greater distance. That had been the plan of the culprits, but only within the farming belt starting at the Monkoo region and ending at the Inosh Mountains. But bird feathers had carried them much farther, and the first signs of spread had begun to manifest themselves near other native territories.

Eradicating the infestation was well above my pedigree. A thorough investigation by the Enforcers of the United Planets Organization failed to prove beyond any doubt that the Conglomerate had been behind it. They had been too smart in covering their tracks. However, everyone knew. While we couldn't officially pin this on them, they still ended up indirectly paying to clear the infestation.

The punitive and exemplary damages they were condemned to pay over their violation of the non-competition and disloyal marketing laws were beyond savage. Most large companies would have gone bankrupt. They obviously tried to appeal the decision, which was rejected. By unanimous decision, the native species voted to expel the Conglomerate from Xecania. The company and all of their affiliates were forbidden to run any kind of business in any way, shape, or form on the planet.

The settlement went to pay for parts of the cleansing of the forest, although the UPO shouldered a lot of the cost through manpower, research, and the development of the remedy. While we were extremely grateful for all of that support, the United Planets Organization wasn't doing this merely out of the goodness of their hearts. Xecania had the potential of becoming the second pantry of the solar system. They wanted to see that happen with durable and clean methods.

It took a little over a month for an army of workers from the UPO to wipe out the fungi in a way that wouldn't negatively impact the ecosystem. Still, we would have to keep an eye out for years to come for its resurgence or the potential appearance of a mutated version.

The fauna slowly returned over multiple months, the smaller critters first. With our newfound wealth, we set up a monitoring and surveillance system that would allow us to detect such disturbances sooner in the future. We also updated the technology in our current houses and bought a small fleet of shuttles —including a large transport ship. With the arrival of our first farmers, these vessels would be put to good use to carry our crops to the spaceport.

We built the human dwellings at a central location between the five clans. With our shuttle fleet, it took the workers barely twenty minutes to reach their destination. It turned out that a few of the third daughters we hired actually had children, a handful of them also having a spouse. In no time, it grew into a comfortable little village, with its own school, restaurant, medical clinic, and a movie theater—that also served as an auditorium—to name a few. We negotiated some deals with the tourist resorts to share acts and entertainment with the village, which reduced costs for all involved.

I couldn't deny that having fellow humans on a regular basis in my life again was nice. I hadn't realized how much I'd missed having a completely nerdy conversation about the best types of natural fertilizers or the latest upgrades to the nanobots used as pesticides. They could be remotely programmed to only target the pest we wanted to eliminate and could be safely removed from the field with a magnetic hoverbot.

In the spirit of slowly opening our people to the more advanced worlds out there, a couple of the human village teachers visited the clans to give tech classes. We also hired a few mentors—especially for Builders like Luped—to show them ways to improve their current techniques, introduce them to better technologies, from wireless networks to heating, and from sprinkler systems to renewable energy.

And the best part of it? All those toys improved our quality of life without changing it. The Andturians had no desire to become the next big metropolis. We had a simple way of life focused on community, providing for each other while ensuring everyone got to do the things that would allow them to thrive physically and intellectually.

Our food trade funneled large amounts of credits that filled the clans' coffers, a massive nest egg for whatever our future generations would want to do. It also allowed us to pay very comfortable wages to our employees, making the farms of Xecania one of the most sought-after workplaces, not just for third-daughter farmers. All the other positions related to transformation—like turning our wheat to flour or our fruits and vegetables to preserves—packaging, shipping, and maintenance had to be filled. Therefore, the village slowly evolved into something more intergalactic instead of just humans. Some members of the native tribes even started working in our facilities.

As was to be expected, a romance blossomed between an Andturian and one of the third daughters. Junit and a lovely woman named Mandy fell for each other while she worked in one of the fields of our village. As I watched Junit's sister and mother take away his soon to be bride to his dwelling to prepare her—as Yamir and Luped had prepared me—I couldn't help but smile. What a long way we'd come in that year…

"They thought I was becoming senile when I told Olix to seek a female from the stars," Molzeg said behind me, startling me.

I turned around to look at the elder female, already adorned to preside over the ceremony.

"In truth, I also wondered if the Spirits weren't playing tricks on me to suggest such a thing," she said pensively. "But the vision was undeniable."

"You saw what would happen?" I asked.

"No, I only saw Olix going through the mating ceremony with a pale-skinned, scaleless female with strings of honey on her head. And the darkness weighing over our villages faded away. Then he brought you here."

"And you wondered how the heck such a fragile little thing was going to save your people," I said teasingly.

Molzeg didn't laugh. A strange expression crossed her

features. "When you let go of his hand, I thought I had made a grievous mistake and misread the signs. I thought I had doomed my people to extinction."

The old female shuddered, a haunted look fleeting over her face. I wanted to say something but realized she wasn't done. I waited patiently while she regained her composure. Her gaze lowered to my swollen belly. My first child would pop out any day now.

"But you held on to him with your right hand," Molzeg said at last. "You held on, and so did he. That's when I knew you would indeed bring the light to the clans. You will never understand the extent of the horrors we endured at the hands of the Vaengi. I still had nightmares about it. You also made them recede back into the shadows where they belong. And now, you bring life. Thank you for giving peace to an old female, and prosperity to a once threatened people."

To my shock, the elder female leaned forward and kissed my forehead. She chuckled at the stunned look on my face.

"You are not the only one who can learn foreign customs," the Seer said teasingly. Her gaze flicked towards Yamir who was gesturing at her. The bride and groom were ready. She turned back towards me. "Time to bind a new human to our clan. I promise not to bruise this one."

I burst out laughing, remembering the brutal sting of the branch she'd whipped me with, not realizing the extent of her strength on my human skin. She winked and headed towards the altar where the ceremony would take place.

OLIX

I was pacing up and down the plaza under the amused glances of my clan. Three hours my Susan had been having contractions but still claimed they were too spaced out for the time being. How would she know? She'd never given birth before, and especially not to an Andturian offspring. Yes, I'd read all the medical literature about human pregnancies. Yes, I understood that she wasn't dilated enough. But this wasn't a human baby. And then she'd kicked me out of the house because I was stressing her out.

What about my stress?

With Andturian females, the minute they got their first contraction, they drank some anetra tea, and the little one would come right out within minutes. Why didn't the human doctor want to let Susan drink that tea? And why wouldn't she let me take my mate to the medical clinic we had built in the workers' village?

"You are wearing out the stones with all that pacing," Zoltar said teasingly.

I hissed at him, which only made him laugh more.

"Your little human has proven to be far stronger than I gave her credit for," my cousin continued, a smile in his voice. "She will deliver a healthy offspring. Stop worrying so much."

"You haven't read and seen all the frightening things that can go wrong with a human pregnancy," I snapped back. "Their females sometimes die, bleed to death, or—"

"Yes, I have," he interrupted, dismissively.

Stunned, I stopped my pacing and turned to look at him, wide eyed.

"We all have," he continued, holding my gaze unwaveringly. "She may have been born human, Susan is one of ours now. She's an Andturian of Monkoo. She's our Clan Mistress. She's my cousin's mate. And she saved our people. We ALL learned what signs of trouble to look out for during her pregnancy, and how to assist if things go poorly. Your mate and your child will be fine."

I gaped at him, speechless. My gaze roamed over the faces of my clanmates gathered on the plaza. They smiled at me, and my throat tightened with emotion.

"We love her, too," Pawis said.

I opened my mouth to respond when my dwelling door opened, and my mother called out to me.

"The baby is coming!" she shouted.

I ran to the house, my heart threatening to beat its way out of my chest. The female doctor had brought a birthing table, which we had installed in one of the guestrooms. Luped and my mother stepped out of the way, leaving room for me to stand by my mate. I slipped my arm around Susan's back to support her, and she held on to my hand with bone crushing strength.

"Push!" the doctor said, standing between my Susan's parted legs.

My female complied with a warrior's cry that turned me into a complete mess. She was in pain, and I was helpless to aid her. She collapsed against me, breathing heavily until the doctor told her to push again. Susan obeyed again. Then something snapped inside of me. My lips parted and a flow of encouragement spilled out of my mouth, just like I'd seen in the videos.

But not their words, my words.

Words about how much I loved her, how she was the strongest of females, how I went to sleep every night, eager for the sun to rise again, just so that I could see her and be with her. That she was my heart, my today, my tomorrow, and my forever. And that she had better push that baby out now because seeing her in pain was messing with me, and not in a good way.

That made her laugh. And then she groaned. And the baby came out.

He was so big, with light green scales with patches of black that would turn out exactly like mine once he grew up. Just by the length of his tail, I already knew our son would be agile and fast, likely a Hunter like his father. Unlike human babies, Andturians didn't cry, they hissed and made rattling or hiccupping sounds to clear their lungs and airways.

The doctor made me cut the umbilical cord and quickly wiped the youngling before handing him over to me. Emotion choking me, I brought our little Gayko to my mate who was both laughing and crying at the same time.

My female still had mixed feelings about the name. We had wanted to honor Kayog for all that he had done behind the scenes not only to bring Susan and me together, but to assist us in regaining control of our lives. Playing around with the letters of his name had given this very nice sounding name. But my mate had objected that it phonetically sounded like an adorable lizard from Earth called a gecko. That sealed it. Clearly, it was a sign from the Spirits. How else could such a coincidence have occurred? She eventually caved when my mother and Luped also sided with me.

Susan looked at our little Gayko in wonder, counting his webbed fingers and toes, and then covering his face with kisses.

"He's perfect, just like you," Susan said in a choked voice. "I love you so much," she added, looking at me, her eyes brimming with tears.

"I love you, too, my Susan," I replied, my heart filling to bursting. "Thank you for choosing me. Thank you for being my greatest blessing."

THE END

OLIX

BOSENGI

ALSO BY REGINE ABEL

THE VEREDIAN CHRONICLES
Escaping Fate
Blind Fate
Raising Amalia
Twist of Fate
Hands of Fate
Defying Fate

BRAXIANS
Anton's Grace
Ravik's Mercy
Krygor's Hope

XIAN WARRIORS
Doom
Legion
Raven
Bane
Chaos
Varnog
Reaper
Wrath
Xenon
Nevrik

PRIME MATING AGENCY
I Married A Lizardman
I Married A Naga
I Married A Birdman
I Married A Minotaur
I Married A Merman

I Married A Dragon

THE MIST
The Mistwalker
The Nightmare

BLOOD MAIDENS OF KARTHIA
Claiming Thalia

VALOS OF SONHADRA
Unfrozen
Iced

EMPATHS OF LYRIA
An Alien For Christmas

THE SHADOW REALMS
Dark Swan

OTHER
True As Steel
Bluebeard's Curse
Alien Awakening
Heart of Stone
The Hunchback

ABOUT REGINE

USA Today bestselling author Regine Abel is a fantasy, paranormal and sci-fi junky. Anything with a bit of magic, a touch of the unusual, and a lot of romance will have her jumping for joy. She loves creating hot alien warriors and no-nonsense, kick-ass heroines that evolve in fantastic new worlds while embarking on action-packed adventures filled with mystery and the twists you never saw coming.

Before devoting herself as a full-time writer, Regine had surrendered to her other passions: music and video games! After a decade working as a Sound Engineer in movie dubbing and live concerts, Regine became a professional Game Designer and Creative Director, a career that has led her from her home in Canada to the US and various countries in Europe and Asia.

Facebook
https://www.facebook.com/regine.abel.author/

Website
https://regineabel.com

Regine's Rebels Reader Group
https://www.facebook.com/groups/ReginesRebels/

Newsletter
http://smarturl.it/RA_Newsletter

Goodreads
http://smarturl.it/RA_Goodreads

Bookbub
https://www.bookbub.com/profile/regine-abel

Amazon
http://smarturl.it/AuthorAMS

Lightning Source UK Ltd.
Milton Keynes UK
UKHW021258090123
415059UK00023B/769